Titles in the *Behold the Eye* trilogy:

*Behold the Eye: Braumaru*

*Behold the Eye: Cerulea*

*Behold the Eye: Viridia*

# *Behold the Eye:*
# *Braumaru*

### *Book 1*

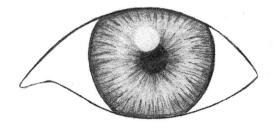

# By Veronica R. Tabares
## Illustrated by Tara Tabares

Sun Break Publishing, Seattle, WA

Published by Sun Break Publishing, 1037 NE 65th St. #164, Seattle, Washington 98115.


Library of Congress Control Number: 2007908711

ISBN: 978-0-9815557-0-6

Publishers note:
This book is a work of fiction and a figment of the author's imagination. Similarities to actual characters, places, names, or events are purely coincidental.

Dedicated to my almost perfect family.

Onny, you are a wonderful husband and I really appreciate all the support you have given me.

Tara, Jade, Elle, and Bridgitt--you four are the best daughters a mother could ever have!

# Braumaru
# Land of the Brown-Eyes

Dear Librarian,

 I am in your library all the time, so you might remember me. I check out several books every week, and I always return them on time. (Except for those two books I'm still paying for. I really didn't know that my little brother was using the books to build a dam. I don't mix books with water, but I guess my little brother is too young to know any better. He's also pretty sneaky. My mom says that it was my fault for leaving the books where he could find them, so I'm paying out of my allowance. I should be finished paying next month.)

 Anyway, the real reason I am writing is because I found a mistake in your library. I found "Behold the Eye: Braumaru" in the fiction section, but it isn't fiction.

 I know that you probably get a lot of people telling you that they think things should be done a certain way, like the library should be decorated a particular way. Or maybe they think it's open the wrong hours and things like that. And I know all about people not wanting certain books in the library, I always pay attention during Banned Books Week.

 But this is different. I really, really know what I am talking about when I say that "Behold the Eye" is not fiction. I know it is true because it is MY story.

To be honest, I can't say that it's just my story, because it is also the story of my friends. (Tricia, Cathy, and Karen have been my friends forever. Micah and Shanti are newer friends. And of course there are also a lot of other people who are important to the story, some are new friends, some are old, and some are most definitely not friends.)

You probably wonder why, since it is my story, that I didn't write the book myself. Well, I tried, but it was too big of a story. Writing a book is a little harder than I first thought. I even tried to get together with my friends to write it. But it turned out that they were too busy. So my friends and I found an author who agreed to write our story into a book for us.

The author warned us that no one would ever believe that it is a real story. She said that everyone would call it a fantasy.

I guess she was right.

But trust me, this stuff really happened!


Sincerely,
Vickie Sutton

Chaos.

Everywhere is chaos. I am scared, tired, and hungry. No one cares if I have fresh water in which to bathe, a warm place to sleep, or even food. No one is in charge, people are missing, and there is no law.

Yet still, it is better than the day of the tragedy. The fires in the forests have finally stopped, and the putrid smell of burning vegetation has begun to go away. I do not know what caused most of my people to disappear, nor do I know how an entire city can vanish without a trace. But I suspect that it has something to do with the shooting stars that hit my city.

# Chapter 1

MICAH BOUNDED UP the stairs two at a time, and leapt into his bed. Gone were the slow, controlled motions that usually characterized all his actions.

Who could move slowly after a day like today? Especially since, or so it seemed to Micah, lightening was coursing through his body instead of blood. Every heartbeat sent energy clear to the tips of each finger, and moving slowly was just not an option.

It had been a very exciting day, although a tiring one. His heart still raced as he thought about the task he had successfully accomplished during the Rite, followed by the ceremony, laughter, games, and light-heartedness he had enjoyed on this day...his day.

But even with the excitement of the day coursing through his body, he could not stop yawning as he snuggled under his covers. It felt so good to relax. The anticipation was finally over. He was now a man, a happy but tired man.

Micah could not believe that this day had finally come. He, Micah Zomorah, was at last a man!

During the ceremonies today, every member of his community had acknowledged his maturity. Every child, woman, and man had hugged him, shaken hands with him, or, as with most of his friends, playfully punched his arm.

He did not even mind that the punches of his closest friends would probably leave bruises for weeks. It was worth it. The Rite of Passage was over, and he had accomplished his chosen task.

Of course, in the minds of many people, he would not be a full-fledged adult until his birth gift manifested itself. But he was not worried; he had only just now turned fifteen. Birth gifts have been known to show themselves at ages as early as 10, and as late as 25. He cared little that he was not going to be one of those early bloomers. It was probably for the best. He had heard of several children whose gifts arrived well before they were old enough to know how to handle them.

Even so, he hoped he would not have to wait until his 20s to discover the nature of his gift. It would be torture to wait that long! Life was always more exciting when you knew what you were supposed to be doing. Waiting was boring.

Still, even though he was not yet prepared to move on to the next phase of his life, he was excited. Childhood was over, even if adulthood had not fully begun. The future was full of unlimited opportunities. All he needed now was to know the form his natural talents would take.

Feeling his body getting heavier and heavier as he relaxed into his mattress, Micah knew he was about to drift off into sleep. Tonight he was happy, and he was not afraid he would have one of his frequent nightmares. His spirits were so high that he knew that even if his dreams were exciting, they would still be pleasant.

He would sleep well.

There is a silence in the air that I cannot become used to. All my life, I have been accustomed to the steady hum of a busy city. I have felt the vibrations of many footsteps, heard the murmur of many voices, had my thoughts cushioned by the presence of the educated. Now, there is an overwhelming stillness, broken occasionally by the presence of the lonely few who have survived.

# Chapter 2

OUT OF THE corner of her eye, Vickie saw a movement outside the fence of the playground.

"I bet that's a dog," Vickie said under her breath. "I just love dogs! If I get to the fence in time, I'll get to pet it."

Vickie turned her head quickly, trying to get a better look at her potential new canine friend before she jumped up and raced to the fence.

"Darn," Vickie mumbled to herself, "no one is there. I guess it's just as well; it probably would have been a snappy little dog instead of a friendly big one."

"But right now," Vickie continued mumbling under her breath, "even a little dog with an inferiority complex would be better than nothing. All we ever do at recess anymore is sit."

It was late in the school year, and the 6th grade girls of Westwood Middle School were tired of all the normal playground activities. Kickball made them sweaty (boys don't like sweaty girls), basketball always messed up a girl's hair, and swings and the Jungle Gym were just too babyish. There was nothing to do at recess!

"I'm bored," said Vickie aloud to her friends, "does anybody have a game we can play?"

When none of the other three girls answered, Vickie decided to take charge of the situation. What she really wanted was excitement, something that not only reflected a sixth-grader's status of near-adulthood, but an adventure so great that it would make a good book.

That was it! Forget about games, she needed to write a book. Vickie devoured books like most kids devoured pizza, and one of her goals was to write a best seller when she grew up.

Well, she thought, why wait? Adults wrote best sellers all the time, and why should they have all the fun! And besides, writing a book sounded like an exciting adventure! At least it could be exciting if she could convince her friends to write it with her.

"Hey guys," Vickie shouted with excitement, "how about we write a book? You know, one of those real life books, about all the cool things that happen in our lives?"

The other girls, shocked out of their lethargy by the extreme loudness of Vickie's voice, looked at her as if she had suddenly grown an extra head. Write a book! Was she nuts? Writing was work, not fun.

"I bet," Vickie continued, lowering her voice to a more normal level now that she had her friends' attention, "if the four of us get together, we could write something so great the whole world would want to buy it. It would be fun, and we could be rich and famous!"

The girls had been sitting in a stupor for most of recess, so no one even thought to speak as the minutes ticked by. Each girl—trying to be fair to her friend—decided to weigh the work of writing against the joy of becoming rich and famous.

The idea of fame and fortune was so appealing, and the dream of becoming world-renowned writers so strong, that the playground around them started to fade off into the distance. They no longer heard the laughter and screams of their fellow classmates enjoying recess all around them.

"I'm so glad you liked my book, your majesty," Tricia mumbled with a bow, as her imagination took her to England to become fast friends with the royal family.

Karen shivered and whispered, "Are there many more ghosts here?" In her mind's eye, fame opened doors to the darkest dungeons and the scariest haunted houses.

"I just love having so many servants," Cathy sighed in contentment. She was thoroughly enjoying her daydream, in which she watched as a retinue of servants cleaned up after one of her many star-studded parties. Cathy's parents believed in the value of chores, and Cathy had quite a few she was expected to do around the house. "My good fellow," Cathy commanded softly to a member of her imaginary staff as she pointed off into the distance, "you must not forget to dust underneath my diamond tiara."

When she became rich and famous, the first thing Cathy was going to do was hire enough help that she would never again be required to lift a finger for housework.

"Alfred, bring me the phone so that I can call the president," Cathy serenely instructed her butler. "I am having a party next week. I shall need you to—ouch!" Her very important call to the president was interrupted when a stray ball from a nearby kickball game crashed into her back.

A ball in the back is as good as a bucket of water over the head to end a daydream. And of course, Cathy wasn't going to let her friends enjoy their daydreams if she wasn't going to get to enjoy hers. She grabbed the ball and tossed it to Tricia, hitting her in the head. The ball bounced off Tricia's head and over to Karen, who came out of her daydream quick enough to catch it and throw it back to the waiting kickball players.

Just as some people wake up in the morning cranky, Tricia woke from her daydream in less than a good mood. A hit to the head with a kickball will sometimes bring out the crankiness in a person. Besides, she had been enjoying her time with the royalty of Europe.

"Writing a book is a cool idea, but I don't see what we would write about," scoffed Tricia as she gingerly rubbed her head to see if she had a bump where the ball had hit her. "Nothing exciting ever happens to us."

Tricia, as Vickie's best friend, should have been enthusiastic about the book idea. The problem was that Tricia hated anything that resembled schoolwork, which she thought was a waste of her time. She was much more likely to spend her energy figuring out which boy in class was the cutest, smartest, nicest, etc.

Karen, who practically lived for scary movies, had been imagining herself living in a haunted castle. A tingle of anticipation raced up and down her spine at the thought. There was no way she would let this opportunity pass her by. Her parents certainly would not be purchasing a haunted castle any day soon. If she wanted to live in one, she would have to do the purchasing. Other than by writing a book, how else could a sixth-grader earn enough money to buy an entire castle!

"Nothing ever happens to us? Are you kidding?" Karen challenged Tricia. "Scary stuff happens all the time. Why just last night I felt the chill hand of a ghost brush across my forehead as I was drifting off to sleep."

"Come on," replied Tricia with a sneer, "Vickie suggested a true life book, not one of your fantasies."

Tricia looked at Karen with disgust. She knew that Karen's vivid imagination could supply many exciting adventures for a book, but none of them would be true adventures. Karen's imagination was even better than Cathy's, and she tended to live in a dream world, one that was over-full of ghosts and goblins.

"I think true life books sell better than fiction books," explained Vickie. "And what we really want to do is sell a lot of books! Karen, do you really think the book should be about spooky things?"

"I know you all think that I imagine things all the time, but I don't," said Karen. "I know there is enough real creepy stuff going on around us that we could write the spookiest book ever. We could write a book that people would buy! People love scary stories, and Vickie, you're right. People love real stories. A book that is scary and real would have to be a best seller."

"Yeah, I read this really great ghost story the other day, and it's a true story. It was so creepy that I had to sleep with my lights on for a week," chimed in Cathy. "Most of the people I know are buying that book, just because it's scary. And I have an aunt that collects books about true ghost stories. You should see how many she has!"

Vickie thought about all the scary books she had read, all the scary movies she had trembled through, and all the scary stories she and her friends had terrorized each other with at slumber parties. A spooky book probably would be a best seller; it seemed that everyone liked to hear about haunted houses, ghosts in the graveyard, and dogs barking at sounds people could not hear.

"Well, it sounds like a really good idea. I'm okay with the spooky book thing, but I really, really, want it to be a real-life story. Now, the truth—does anything scary ever really happen to us?" Vickie questioned her friends sternly.

I dreamed of my brother and sister last night. It seemed so real that it hurt when my sister pinched me. I even have a bruise in the same spot!

It was so comforting to once again feel that I belonged. We played games and teased each other, just like old times.

Only after I awoke did I recall that they were truly gone, and have been for 2 seasons. My dreams are now the only place where I will be able to see my loved ones. How will I learn to live with my loneliness? How will I continue to survive, all alone, no family, no friends, and none of my servants to take care of me?

*Chapter 3*

W ITH A START, Micah sat up in his bed, his heart pounding in his chest. The moonlight shining in his window, as well as the cool night air, let him instantly be aware that it was still the middle of the night. Why had he woken up, and why did he feel so frightened?

Micah tiptoed into his parent's bedroom and gently shook his father's shoulder. "Father," Micah whispered, "I have had a dream that is very strange."

Normally, Micah would not have awakened his father for anything as trivial as a dream. But Micah's parents had stressed that they needed to immediately know about anything unusual that happened after the ceremony.

Yawning, his father sat up in bed. Looking at Micah's sleeping mother, he motioned Micah to move into the next room. There was no reason for both parents to get up in the middle of the night.

"Was it another of your terror dreams?" the sleepy Zebulan questioned his son.

"No, it was not a terror dream. In truth, it was a very boring dream. There were four girls just sitting on the ground talking. I was...I was quite a distance away, so I could not even hear of what they were saying. Nothing really happened except one girl got hit in the head with a ball, and she was not even hurt."

Zebulan stretched both of his hands over his head as he yawned, and tried to keep his eyes focused on his son. He had enjoyed the day of activities celebrating his son's maturity, but he was exhausted. He tried to push the thought of the comfortable bed waiting for him in the next room out of his mind.

"Micah, it is unlike you to awaken me from my slumber, unless you have a good reason. What of this dream makes you worry?"

"In truth Dad, I do not know what of the dream bothered me. But when one of the girls looked at me, I sensed a kinship with her. She seemed to see me no more than she would see the wind on an open field, yet I felt a shock of recognition. I should know this girl. I was disappointed that she failed to see me."

"A shock of recognition? Mayhap this girl has a gift similar to your own, whatever your gift turns out to be. Do you think that you have seen her before? Was she at the ceremony?"

"No Father, I am certain that I have never seen any of those girls before. Their dress and mannerisms were funny, and very odd to me. And this dream felt like no other. I had no ability to interact. I was there to watch, but not to take part. Never before have I been restricted thus in my dreams, even in my terror dreams."

Zebulan knew that Micah's terror dreams usually featured either himself or Micah's mother, and usually they ended with the death of a parent. Zebulan also knew that children often had terror dreams of this sort; it was just a way to work through fears.

Micah looked at his father. It was only fair, after waking him from a sound sleep, to tell him what was really bothering him about these dreams.

"Father, I have never before had a dream such as this one. All my dreams are of familiar places and people. Tonight I dreamed of strangers in a strange place. But this somehow did not seem odd to me, instead it felt comfortable and real. I fear this change in my dreams. I fear the unfamiliar feeling familiar, and the unreal feeling real."

Zebulan listened quietly to his son. Micah had never been the type of child to worry unnecessarily. He had always been an easygoing, even-tempered, rather serene child. There was no reason to think that the Rite of Passage would change the nature of Micah's personality. If something was worrying Micah, there was probably something to worry about. Zebulan struggled to try to understand what was bothering his son.

"There is more, Father. When I suffer through a terror dream, I awake sitting up in my bed and breathing quickly, as if I had been running a great distance. The fear I feel during the dream makes it so. Tonight I awoke in just such a manner. But there was nothing to fear in the dream. No terrifying cliffs to fall from, no loved one in danger, no burning buildings in which to be trapped. Why would I awake from a dream, a boring dream which has nothing in it to fear, as if it were a dream full of terror?"

"Micah, my son," Zebulan replied with a sigh, "I do not have the answer to your question. Let us go back to sleep for this night, and talk of this again on the morrow. In the morn, our minds will not be as cluttered with the cobwebs of slumber. Maybe then I will be able to answer your question."

Micah nodded in agreement, hugged his father, and returned to his room, deciding not to worry any more for that night. Lying back down, Micah rolled over onto his side and closed his eyes. He was so exhausted that he knew that going to sleep was not going to be a problem.

As he drifted back to sleep, the picture of the four girls sitting in a circle talking kept intruding into his thoughts. Was he going to dream of them again?

Every day that goes by makes the weight of my loss just a bit lighter. The pain is lessening, but slowly, oh so slowly. Each day, it is a struggle to rise and face the day. Nevertheless, I have learned to accept that I will no longer be able to challenge my brother to a game of Chomka, or tease my sister about her hair.

My parents, I miss not as much. I had accepted the loss of my parents long ago. I so rarely saw them. They were at all times much too busy to play with their children.

I know I should rejoice that I was spared. But sometimes I wonder. . . was I really fortunate to be out of the city on that day. I feel so alone, so different from everyone around me. I think I am the only one remaining of my status, the only one with any sort of education. If I had not gone out to check on the workers and update the logbooks, would I have disappeared like everyone else?

Where did all my family and friends go?

# Chapter 4

PROFESSOR MELISSA JAMISON stopped suddenly, disrupting the river of students rushing down the hallway. She was so intent on her discovery that she did not notice that the students were now forced to flow around her much as water flows around a stone placed in the middle of a stream.

"How could I not have seen this before," Professor Jamison whispered to herself, as she often did when she needed to concentrate in a noisy environment. "I've looked at this book a thousand times, but I never noticed this writing in the margins."

Of course, Professor Jamison knew why she had never noticed the writing before. The writing was so faint that it could only be seen in bright sunlight. No archaeologist in their right mind would expose an ancient artifact like this book to the destructive rays of the sun. Only a chain of unusual events had led to the discovery.

The book had been unearthed during an archaeological field school more than 60 years ago, but had lain untouched in storage until its discovery three months ago. The field school had ended abruptly due to the mysterious disappearance of the professor in charge of the field school, and all the other archaeologists at the university at the time had been much too busy with their own work to want to take on the work of another professor.

Three months previously, a water pipe had broken in the archaeology lab, leaving two inches of water on the floor. The pipe was fixed and the water cleaned up quickly, but not before the moisture had created the perfect growing environment for several types of mold. The mold proved so difficult to get rid of that the only option was to move everything out of the lab and into a dry storage area.

It was during the move that the forgotten artifacts from that long ago field school were discovered. Professor Jamison, as the head of the archaeology lab, felt that it was her responsibility to clean and catalog the artifacts. After all, she thought, if no one knows that the artifacts exist, they are rather hard to study.

Books are a rare find at an archaeological site, so Professor Jamison began her cataloging under the assumption that the book had belonged to the professor in charge of the dig. It was only after she was through with all the other artifacts that she even took the time to open the book. She quickly became excited because of its obvious age, and not in the least disappointed in its content. Books of this age, of which there were very few, were quite often dry texts listing supplies owned by a community. These lists provided useful information about the day-to-day lifestyles of that community. Archaeologists simply love to discover books of this sort.

That had been a month ago, and the book would have still been protected in the new location had not a second pipe burst, this time in the temporary archaeology lab. Once again, all the artifacts needed to be moved.

Professor Jamison left much of the moving to her students, but decided to personally transport the rare book to her dry-as-a-bone office. It was as she walked down the sunny hallway that she made her discovery, a discovery that would not have been made under the artificial lights commonly used throughout the labs in the university.

The words, written in the margin next to a list of seashells that had been traded for baskets, seemed to have no relation to anything else on the page. Professor Jamison reread the words aloud, and continued onto the next page to read the message she discovered there in the margin, her voice rising in excitement. She ignored the mass of humanity rushing past her just as most of the people in the sunny, but crowded, hallway ignored her.

*It is odd that of the people that disappeared, there remains no trace. And it is not only people who have vanished. Whole buildings, along with everything in them, are now as if they had never existed.*

Professor Jamison did not notice the eavesdropper that overheard her every word. She was so focused on her discovery, that she was unaware of the intent attention directed her way as she continued toward her office, her eyes never leaving the pages of the ancient text.

And so, because of a chain of unforeseen events, lives were about to be drastically altered. If the water pipes had not burst, the ancient book might have lain in the lab undiscovered indefinitely. If the sun had not been shining or Professor Jamison had not continued to study the book as she walked down the bright hallway, the hidden message might have remained hidden forever. If Professor Jamison had taken the time to lift her eyes long enough to notice the figure that now shadowed her down the hallway, many of the events now set in motion might not have occurred at all.

Later that night, as the moon shone full and bright on the campus grounds, a shadow moved noiselessly through the darkened hallways of the college. No one was around to see the shadow approach Professor Jamison's office door, or to hear the scrape of metal against metal as a key was inserted into the lock.

As the door of the office creaked open, the silhouette exposed by the dim nightlight in the professor's office gave no clue to the intruder's identity. All that would have been seen, if anyone had been crazy enough to be in the campus building at 2 am, was a figure in a hooded sweatshirt and baggy blue jeans.

Without any further sound, the figure slid into the office and gently closed the door. Only the flashes of light escaping through the crack at the bottom of the door disturbed the serenity of the night.

Several hundred people have gathered together now. They are all laborers and farmers. Even though I do not belong with these people, I cannot stand living all alone. I would have never been friendly with any of this group before the tragedy. Now they are all I have.

# Chapter 5

HUDDLED OVER A cup of espresso, the figure in the gray-hooded sweatshirt stared intently at a camera lying on the table. The sweatshirt, which was large and bulky, camouflaged most details that might have helped identify the figure. That the figure was slender could be surmised by the slimness of the blue jean covered legs crossed at the ankle beneath the chair. The hood, pulled up to cover all of the head and part of the face, gave the mysterious figure almost total anonymity. It was even impossible to tell for sure if the figure was a male or a female. What was easy to tell was that the figure seemed almost unaware of the constant stream of commuters rushing into the coffee shop to get their morning jolt of caffeine.

"If this does not work, I might never get home," the figure said with a grumble. "He said if I used this machine like he showed me, he would be able to read the messages with none knowing. I hope he is right. I want to go home. There are so many things here I do not understand. I know I do not understand these people, who are so unfriendly and distant."

The figure reached out to the camera on the table, and pushed one side. It moved about an inch. Another push, this time to the other side, still only resulted in a slight movement of the camera. It was apparent that the camera was not reacting as desired.

"Come on, show the book to me," whispered the figure. "I do not trust him, and I do not trust this place. I need to find my way home."

No one in the coffee shop paid the slightest attention to the figure sitting in the corner, talking quietly and occasionally poking the camera. No one really cared that the figure was lost and far from home. Everyone was too busy with his or her own life to pay much attention to a stranger. Besides, people in the city usually ignore anyone or anything that might be considered weird or unusual. It was safer that way.

"By the word, he said that to get the book into this machine, I would need to look through this little window until I saw the page of the book, and then press this button. The flash of light meant that the page of the book was copied inside the machine. But how do you get the book back out?"

Pushing the hood of the sweatshirt back, the figure was finally revealed as a girl in her late teens. She was a pretty girl with long brown hair and delicate features. She looked very much like many other girls that could be found in the city. The only truly unusual things about her were an indefinable exotic quality and her eyes. One was blue, and the other brown.

Of course, most other girls in the city knew how they got where they were. This girl had not a clue. She had gone to sleep one night, had a few crazy dreams, and found herself somehow transported from her familiar world of loving family and friends, to this scary world of strange people who seemed to only care about themselves.

She was fortunate that she had always had the ability to learn quickly and blend in. She was familiar with the concept of money, so it took very little time for her to learn how much was needed for what things. He had given her some money; he had many errands he wanted her to do all around the city.

It was funny that everything seemed to come back to him. He was the first person she had seen after waking on that day when she found herself in this strange place. He was in that last strange dream. He said that he was the only one who could help her get back home again.

Her gut feeling told her that he was the last person she should trust. The more she was around him the more she felt he might be a little mentally unbalanced.

Unfortunately, he was the only halfway familiar figure in this strange place of even stranger people. She had no choice but to follow his advice, even if she did not really trust him. Unless, that is, she could figure out how to get back home by herself.

With a sigh, she focused again on her current problem. She knew that there was something in the book that he wanted, and if she could get to it first, maybe she could find her own way home.

"By the word, if the window on this side puts the book in, maybe the one on the other side gets it back out. I will have to try to look in the other side window, to see if I will be able to see into the machine."

She sat up straight in her chair as she scooted slightly away from the table. With her arms held out straight in front of her, she gingerly picked up the camera.

"I sure hope this works," she said with a sigh. She did not want to admit to herself that she was a little afraid of the machine. If it could copy the book, could it copy her? If it did, would it hurt?

Slowly, she moved the camera closer to her face until her eye was even with the shutter.

"Nothing...I cannot see a single thing," she said with frustration. "How do I make this thing work?"

Remembering the button she had pushed to copy the book, she decided to try pushing it now. She opened her eyes as wide as possible, and looked intently into the window that she hoped would give her a look at the book. It was too important that she learn everything she could before she gave the machine to him for her to give up yet.

Taking a deep breath, she pushed the button. The light flashed just above her head, and she saw the jaws of the machine open and close quickly, barely missing her eye. Startled, she jerked the camera away from her face and gently put it back on the table. Was the machine angry that she was trying to learn its secrets?

No longer willing to experiment with the dangerous machine after it snapped at her eye, the girl decided that she must trust him, this man who had promised to help her get back to her home. Feeling somewhat defeated, she finished her coffee with a gulp. The sooner she got the machine to him, the quicker he could get the information he needed to send her back home.

As the survivors of my kingdom continue to gather together, I discover just exactly how tragic our days have become. Only the people either traveling or out in the fields at the time of the disaster are still here. All families have lost at least one loved one, and in many cases, entire families have disappeared. I seem to be the only member of my family left. I used to feel proud to be a member of the royal family, but what good is that pride now.

# Chapter 6

WRITING A BOOK was a lot harder than the four friends had expected. As a matter of fact, finding out what to write about was a lot harder than expected.

The four girls were convinced that their lives could not possibly be as boring as they seemed; after all, they knew in their hearts that they were destined for greatness. So it was agreed that they would each open themselves to the "forces around them", and make a note of anything that could be thought of as spooky, weird, or unusual. They would then meet and collect it all together. When they had enough material for a book, they would write their bestseller and become instantly famous.

After a week of observations, the girls discovered they had collected four ghostly shadows (shaped strangely like little brothers), five pieces of candy mysteriously missing (again, little brothers were implicated), and one dream that appeared to have visited all four girls on the same night.

Vickie, who was the official note taker, threw down her notebook in disgust.

"This isn't working. Shadows and missing candy; is that the best we can do?"

"But what about the dream?" questioned Cathy. "Isn't it strange that we all had the same dream?"

"Yes, all of us having the same dream on the same night certainly seems weird, except I don't believe we really did. Somebody is cheating."

As she noticed the offended expressions on her friends' faces, Vickie decided to soften her criticism. "I mean, how do we know that all four of us had the same dream? You know how hard dreams are to remember. Maybe once we heard about Tricia's dream, our memories changed to match our dream to hers."

The four girls were meeting on the playground at recess again. Even though the sun was shining and there were happy children playing all around them, the four were feeling the dejection of a plan gone wrong. Karen kicked a loose rock that was handy at her foot, and it flew right at Vickie and bounced off her shoe.

"This isn't going to work," complained Karen. "We need to be more scientific about this, so that we can really back up the facts in our book!"

Tricia cleared her throat importantly. It was hard not to smirk, but she must control herself and set a good example. To think that all her friends had copied her dream. But Karen was right, to do the book right, there could be no cheating.

"I have a great idea," suggested Tricia, "from now on, we'll write down every dream, every morning. Then we'll get together and switch papers with each other. That way we'll know that there are no mistakes, and that no one is cheating!"

Vickie looked around at her friends, pleased by the eager nods of agreement she saw. Finally, progress! She didn't want to publish a book based on lies, and she certainly could not figure out which spooky occurrences were lies and which the truth by herself. She and her friends needed to get their act together.

"So," questioned Vickie, mimicking her mother's sternest 'you better take me seriously' look, "are we all agreed there will be no cheating? And that we have to stick to the facts?"

Three heads nodded an affirmative.

"Then lets swear on a solemn oath," continued Vickie.

The four girls stood in a circle and placed their right hands together in the middle of the circle.

"Repeat after me," said Vickie in her most serious voice. "I solemnly swear to only tell the truth."

"I solemnly swear to only tell the truth," echoed the three friends.

Karen slapped at her leg with her right hand, breaking the bond of hands.

"Put your hand back in, we're not finished," snapped Tricia.

"I couldn't help it, a mosquito bit me," Karen explained with a scowl. She scratched at her leg, hating the itchy feeling that comes with a mosquito bite.

"Well, can't you at least put your right hand back in and scratch with your left?" questioned Tricia in her bossiest and most aggravating tone.

"Fine," said Karen. "I can't reach the mosquito bite with my left hand, but for the sake of our book, I'll suffer through the itchies."

Scrunching up her face to show the pain she was suffering for the group, Karen shoved her right hand back into the circle. "You can go ahead now."

"Where was I? Oh yes. Now say…about all the mysterious and creepy things in my life," Vickie continued.

"About all the mysterious and creepy things in my life," the three girls chanted. Karen twisted her body around, trying to get her left hand to reach around her body so she could scratch the back of her right leg, while still keeping her right hand in the circle. No success.

"So that we can write the best and most truthful book ever," finished Vickie, glaring at Karen to make her stop wiggling.

"So that we can write the best and most truthful book ever," repeated Tricia, Cathy, and Karen.

"Wait," yelled Tricia suddenly, just as the friends were about to release the bond their hands had made. The girls were so startled by her outburst that they instantly froze, even Karen who had just sighed in relief that she was about to end the torture of the itchy mosquito bite on her leg.

Tricia continued in a thoughtful voice, "We need a penalty if someone breaks the oath. Add...."

Tricia paused to try to think of the worst penalty a person could have for lying to the group. A slow smile spread across her face as inspiration hit.

Karen could barely control the urge to scratch, but she knew that if she made a move, the four friends would probably remain standing in this circle all day. Tricia was one of those people who the more you hurried, the slower they became. A few more minutes of itchy torment now would soon become scratching bliss very soon, if Karen could just stay still. After all, how long does it take to take a solemn oath?

Vickie and Cathy waited patiently for Tricia to continue. They recognized that slightly wicked smile, and knew it meant that Tricia had thought up a truly horrendous punishment for whoever dared to break the rules.

This was going to be dangerously good.

"On pain of losing our friendship," Tricia solemnly finished, saying each word slowly and emphasizing the words pain and friendship.

"On pain of losing our friendship," Vickie, Cathy, and Karen parroted back to her. A shiver ran down each girl's spine. Nothing was worse than losing your best friends.

The girls broke their circle, feeling a little scared about the oath, but over all more in control of the future. An oath was a serious thing, and none of the girls had any intention of taking it lightly.

There were several minutes of silence as each girl was lost in thought. Exactly how would the oath help to get any writing done? After all, writing the book was what it was all about. Karen looked at her friends, took a deep breath, and decided that now was the time to push this fact-finding venture up to the next level. After all, the book was not going to sell unless it was full of really good, really spooky stuff.

"This oath is great," Karen began, "but dreams are so boring, and the shadows and missing candy are probably our little brothers playing jokes on us. Can't we do something else? You know, isn't there some way we can create a real-life scary story?"

So the girls put their heads together one more time and decided on a new and better plan.

I believe I can rebuild my kingdom. There are many more survivors than I first thought. I know it can be done. I will do everything within my power to make it so.

# Chapter 7

VICKIE HEARD THE young traveler ask, "Have they always lived here? I have never seen so many cobras in one place!"

The reason for the question was obvious. Vickie could see that at least a hundred cobras, startled by a loud explosion, were racing across the grassy field toward the water. As they reached the embankment, they almost flew down to the water, straight into the group of women who had gathered to wash laundry along the shore. Instead of screaming, the women each reached down and scooped up a couple of cobras, draping them around their necks.

With a sudden realization, Vickie understood that she was a spectator in a dream. She had just that night completed her report on the behavior of cobras, and was prepared to present it in her science class the next day. Because of this, she knew that humans and cobras did not coexist in harmony. After all of the facts she had learned about cobras—especially how poisonous their venom was—she knew that the women should have been running away from the cobras, not wearing them as necklaces.

"For as long as anyone can remember, we have had cobras in our village," wheezed a very old man. "Yes, we have always had cobras."

"But how do you protect yourself from the poison?" queried the young man. "In Braumaru, where I am from, I have never seen anything like this. There are so many snakes here. Have your people developed an antidote to the poison?"

The old man turned to the young traveler, looked deep into his eyes, and hooted, "Knew you must not be a green-eye. Boy, what are you thinking about? These snakes would never harm us. Our town was founded by a green-eye, and we have the green-eye gifts. We have never had a snake bite a resident. And never will!"

Vickie turned to the old man and asked, "What does the color of your eyes have to do with it?"

As if he did not hear Vickie, the old man continued. "Yes, we have always had cobras in our village. Cobras are much better than cats at catching mice and rats, and they never cough up hairballs. Nasty things, hairballs."

The old man shuffled off, shaking his head and chuckling softly to himself.

With a shrug, the young traveler turned to continue his journey down the road. Catching sight of Vickie, he stopped suddenly, and cautiously began to move in her direction.

"Hello, my name is Micah," the young traveler said with a shy smile, wondering why this girl looked so familiar.

"Hi there, I'm Vickie."

"High there? Are you…I mean, do you live here?" Micah came to a stop just a foot in front of the girl, and stared at her intently.

"Well," Vickie explained, "since this is a dream, I guess I would have to say I don't live around here. Or maybe I should say I do, since I am probably lying in my own bed."

Micah gulped and asked in a shocked voice, "Did you say…did you say…dream?"

"Of course dream! You know…" Vickie paused and cocked her head as if she were listening for some distant sound. "Oh, I have to go now! I think my mother is calling me. It was nice meeting you, whoever you are!" Vickie yelled as she began to run.

Micah watched Vickie move quickly to one of the nearby houses and dash around to the back yard. He knew he had never met the girl, but she certainly reminded him of someone.

And what had she meant by that curious remark about this being a dream?

With a jerk, Vickie woke up. Wow, she thought, that was so weird it was just short of a nightmare. But it was way too cool to be a nightmare, and way too vivid to be a normal dream!

Vickie was on her side with her head almost buried by her pillow. She knew the time, because the numbers on her alarm clock beside her bed glowed an eerie green 12:05.

Vickie hated the dark, and refused to get up to go to the bathroom or get a drink of water once the lights in the house were turned out for the night. Even though she denied it to everyone else, to herself she admitted that she was afraid of the dark. But as she awoke this night, she felt no fear. Instead, a strange calmness gently settled over her body, soothing her nerves and making her feel that she was protected.

Odd, thought Vickie, I feel as if someone were watching over me, protecting me.

Vickie rolled over onto her stomach, and snuggled deeper into her covers. She felt so warm and protected; she knew she would have no problem going back to sleep, and returning to her fascinating dream.

Glancing up at her headboard, Vickie froze. There, floating a foot above her bed was a giant, fluorescent, orange eye. It glowed in the same way her alarm clock glowed, but with no wires.

Surprisingly unalarmed, Vickie continued to gaze at the eye in wonder. Where did it come from, why was it in her room, what was it? As these questions drifted through her mind, she studied the eye. It appeared almost solid, yet she felt that if she tried to touch it, her hand would go right through.

Vickie had no intention of touching the eye. Her instincts, which she had been taught to trust, warned her that the eye was there to protect her, but also that it was off limits.

With a mental shrug, Vickie once again snuggled into her blankets, closed her eyes, and drifted off to sleep.

"Behold the Eye," whispered a voice in the darkness outside Vickie's window. "The Eye of Janu only watches over those who have untrained power, power that I might be able to use."

"How can that little girl have any power? She is much too young," a slim figure in the hooded jacket whispered back.

"Our world is not like your world. Most people here do not believe in the natural gifts that you have been taught to cherish from birth. Here the gifts would be thought of as magic, as something that is either all trickery or somehow evil. Because of this, my world contains many people with untrained gifts. I have been searching for just the right person, and I think this girl will perfect for my uses."

"You will not hurt her? You promised me that no one would be hurt."

"Hurt? No...she will feel no pain. Besides, you should not concern yourself with someone who is not even of your world. Cooperate, and I will return you to your people."

The two shadows moved away from Vickie's window, while Vickie slept on, oblivious to the danger lurking just outside.

I tried to motivate the survivors to recreate our civilization. I do not know why, but many of the people refuse to rebuild. They say that we must not go back to our old way of living. They say we must forget about great buildings and large cities, and live a simpler life. They think that collecting nuts, berries, and fishing are worth more to our survival than creating a strong, cohesive society. Can they not see that if we want to regain our civilization, we must rebuild as soon as possible?

# Chapter 8

WHISPERING EXCITEDLY, VICKIE said, "Tricia, look! It moved, it really moved. Did you see it?"

Calmly, Tricia stopped focusing on her rock, and turned her attention to Vickie.

"Do it again," she said, "I think I saw it move, but I'm not sure. Remember, we want to be scientific. If you can't do it more than once, you might as well not have done it at all."

Vickie knew that Tricia was right. After all, they had agreed to only use true-life experiences in their book. True-life experiences that they could prove had actually happened.

It was quite a surprise to the girls to find that the hard part was not so much proving the experiences, as finding them in the first place. Finally, out of desperation, they had decided not to wait for the scariness and strangeness to come to them. They would go out and find it, or if necessary, create it.

The rules they set up for themselves were simple, and designed to prevent "cheating". Each girl was to try to find something exciting, unusual, or creepy in her life. They would "work" on the discovery to learn to control whatever the thing was. They did not need to develop full control over the phenomenon, only enough so that they could prove to the others it existed.

For example, Karen was convinced her grandfather, who was also her next-door neighbor, had a ghost in his house. In order to make the ghost part of the girls' story, Karen needed to make friends with it. Since she figured the ghost was probably a relative of some sort, the house and land had been in her family for generations, this did not bother her in the least. Her assignment was to see and talk to the ghost every day, and to learn when and where it was most likely to appear. Then the girls must all have the opportunity to visit the ghost. Only when the ghost's existence was proven beyond a doubt to the group could it become a part of their best seller.

Vickie had always had déjà-vu type dreams, in which she would see parts of her future life. Unfortunately, the fact that she saw things in advance was just too hard to prove. Every time she told her friends about one of her predictions, they always thought she had found a way to cheat. So instead, she decided to teach herself how to move objects with mind power. Having the ability to move objects with her mind would definitely be the sort of skill that would lead to great adventures. Great adventures always make great stories. Great stories written into books usually became best sellers. A best seller would bring fame and fortune to the four friends. Vickie would be a hero.

When Vickie told the other three her plan (leaving out the hero part), all the girls became instantly excited.

"Oh, I want to try!" Cathy exclaimed.

"Me too," Karen cried. "My ghost is not cooperating very well, and I might need to find something else."

"Here," Tricia said, "Let's try to move these rocks." She bent over and scooped up a handful of acorn-sized rocks that the girls sometimes used to play hopscotch while waiting for the bus.

"You mean, right now? You want us to do this at the bus stop, with all these other people around?" Vickie questioned, a little miffed. She really did not want the other girls to try to move objects with their minds; this was her project. Wasn't it just like Tricia to take over and start bossing everyone around? Tricia was Vickie's best friend, but sometimes she was a little hard to put up with.

"Sure, why not. No one will know what we are doing," Tricia answered calmly. Vickie thought she looked a little smug.

Tricia, with her innate bossiness, had the girls sitting on the sidewalk in a circle in no time flat. The girls had each chosen their favorite squashed gumball shaped rock from the collection in Tricia's hand, and placed it directly in front of them. Since the rocks were on a hard flat surface, without even a touch of wind to help them roll, the girls knew that if the rocks moved at all, it could only be by brain power.

After several moments of pure concentration, Vickie lifted her eyes to see if any of her schoolmates was watching the group. She saw Karen sneakily nudge her rock with her shoe, attempting to set it in motion the easy way. Karen's rock stayed firm on the ground. It would take more than a little nudge to move her flat-bottomed rock even the tiniest bit. Why in the world did Karen pick such a flat rock? It was probably the most squished of the squished gumball shaped rocks.

Didn't she realize that it was much easier to make round objects roll?

All the other kids at the bus stop appeared to be occupied. Two girls, a little older than Vickie and her friends, were busily completing homework they had neglected to do the night before. Several of the younger boys had moved over into a yard, and were perfecting their wrestling moves. No one was paying the least attention to Vickie's group.

Vickie felt relief when she discovered that no one at the bus stop was paying the least attention to her group. The last thing she wanted was to have one of these kids questioning what the group was doing. They would probably spread it all over school that Vickie and her friends were nuts, and everyone would laugh at them. Vickie's relief that she and her friends were being ignored allowed her to relax enough that her mind started to drift.

As if a TV had been clicked on in her mind, Vickie suddenly saw the vivid images of a woman turning the pages of a book. The woman looked calm and serene, and her arms were resting on the table about six inches on each side of a dictionary-sized manuscript. No part of her body was in contact with the book, and Vickie knew that the woman was using her thoughts to turn the pages. As Vickie relaxed into the vision, her rock wobbled.

It was at this point that Vickie had whispered in excitement to Tricia.

At Tricia's encouragement, Vickie made the decision to prove then and there that she was able to do this. No one else in the group had been able to move their rocks so much as a wiggle. Vickie knew she had made the rock move, and if she had done it once, she could certainly do it again. Being able to move objects with her mind would make her into a star within her group, and really set the stage for some wonderful adventures for their book. Besides, thought Vickie, just think of the possibilities for practical jokes!

Concentrating as hard as she could, Vickie threw her thoughts into the rock lying placidly on the hard concrete sidewalk. Doubts intruded as she tried to recreate the method she had seen the woman in her vision use just a few minutes previously, but she mentally shoved those doubts aside. As her concentration increased, Vickie realized that what had started as a vision had turned into a feeling. She was no longer sitting on the cold hard sidewalk with schoolmates talking and playing around her, but she was becoming a part of the rock. She began to feel snug in her small, confined space, and perfectly at home on the hard sidewalk.

Okay, thought Vickie, I am in the rock. Or maybe, I am the rock. No matter, now I just need to imagine I am rolling down a hill.

Tricia, as the self-appointed judge, noticed Karen once again trying to cheat and glared at her. After checking on Cathy to assure herself that she wasn't trying to nudge her rock with her shoe instead of her mind, she turned her body to more fully face Vickie. If Vickie really could move the rock with her mind, she wanted to see it, and to be able to say definitively that there had been no cheating.

"Hurry, the bus is coming." Tricia prompted gently, speaking softly so she would not startle Vickie out of her trancelike state. "Concentrate."

Vickie broke into a sweat as she tensed her muscles, just as she would if she were preparing to roll down a big hill. Closing her eyes to increase her concentration, she moved ever so slightly forward, imagining herself starting to roll. As soon as she had the feeling of rolling firmly implanted in her head, she once again opened her eyes and focused her attention on the rock.

Just as the school bus pulled up to the curb, the rock began to roll away from Vickie. It did not stop until it came to rest against the Tricia's shoe, and Tricia's stunned, open-mouthed amazement showed that she really did not believe that Vickie would succeed in her mind-moving-matter project.

"Hey, you weren't touching it!" exclaimed Karen. "How did you do that?"

"You actually moved that rock with your mind," said Cathy in a shocked voice. "That is truly spooky. Listen, I think we all should keep practicing, so that we all learn how to do it. Then we can— "

"Yeah," Karen interrupted with a mischievous gleam in her eye, "Just think how cool it will be, we can use our power to get back at our little brothers for all the weird things they do to us. Can you imagine how scared they will be when their school books fly across the room and land in their lap just when they tell our parents that they don't have any homework?"

So it was decided. Every day while waiting for the bus, each girl was to focus on moving a rock placed on the sidewalk. A little practice each day would surely strengthen their mental muscles. If Karen had her way, soon schoolbooks would fly through the air in all their houses, probably hitting little brothers in the head.

Just before placing her foot on the bottom step of the bus, Vickie spotted a movement out of the corner of her eye. Turning her head quickly, she was just in time to see a shadow disappear from the middle of a yard.

That's strange, thought Vickie. How could there be a shadow in that yard? There are no telephone poles or people around to cast a shadow. Not noticing that she was blocking the other kids from entering the bus, she stopped to stare at the yard. She shivered as she realized there was absolutely nothing around that could have made a shadow in that yard, not even a dog or a cat. Who or what had been there?

A raindrop landed with a plop on Vickie's nose at the same moment that Tricia, who was directly behind her, shoved her up the steps. Tricia spent too much time on her hair in the mornings to worry about manners when rain started to fall. Wet hair just was not her best look.

Micah stretched as he awoke from his dream. Did other people have such realistic dreams? Did other people dream of the same people night after night?

This dreaming business was getting crazier and crazier. These dreams about the four girls in a circle were not exactly the exciting type of dream he normally enjoyed, although at least they were not scary like his nightmares. Still, he might as well dream about taking a test in school, these dreams were so boring.

Except…these dreams felt so real. In this one, he could even smell the scent of rain in the air.

I worry about my people. We had so much knowledge, so much culture, and so many inventions to help us. We were a powerful and wonderful civilization.

Now, all of our leaders are gone, and those inventions are nowhere to be found.

Is there anyone left who knows how to help us rebuild?

Tomorrow I will quest for knowledge.

# Chapter 9

A S MICAH LOOKED to his right, he saw in the distance two girls running through the field, looking over their shoulders to see if they were still being chased. Their mouths were slightly open as they struggled to breathe, and sweat was beginning to bead on their faces. Micah did not know who or what they were running from, he just knew that they had the terrified look of deer running from hunters.

As he calmly watched the girls—wondering what would happen next—Micah realized that he had seen these same two girls before. Their clothing was not the type worn in his region, but he had the uneasy feeling that he knew these two girls very well. Micah racked his memory, trying to place names to their faces. Surely he would be able to recall where and when he had seen them before, and why he felt he should know them as well as he knew his own sisters.

A flood of memories poured into Micah's consciousness from out of the blue, and he remembered that they were two of the girls he had been dreaming about so much lately. Usually there were four girls, and he typically saw them sitting in a circle. He had never actually seen them moving across the landscape before. This dream seemed like it would be more interesting than the usual ones he had about the girls. He might even enjoy this dream if it provided an opportunity to view some excitement from a safe distance.

Without warning, an intense feeling of panic washed over Micah, causing his pulse to race and sweat to form on his brow. He no longer found himself observing from a distance, but running right behind the girls. Even though he knew there was no logical reason, Micah felt compelled to join the girls in their frantic race across the meadows. He was now an unwilling participant in the dream.

Fear consumed him and drove out all thought. This fear was more powerful than any he had ever experienced; so extreme that his heart was racing so fast he thought it might burst at any moment. Just when he thought the feeling of terror could not become any more intense; he saw the blond girl trip and fall, taking the brown-haired girl down with her. His heart jumped up into his throat and he found himself holding his breath, as if the act of breathing would speed the girls' pursuer closer.

Fortunately, the girls were quick to rise and continue running, fear giving them the energy they needed to continue to race across what appeared to be a never-ending field. As Micah once again drew in much needed oxygen, he realized he was so close to the brown haired girl he could have reached out and touched her, but doing that might slow them both down and allow their pursuer to gain ground. With that thought the realization hit him that he did not even know from what danger they were running.

As if from a great distance, Micah began to hear a rhythmic pounding sound, overlaid by a raspy buzz. It stayed in the distance for only a few seconds before the sound rushed into his head with the force of a waterfall that temporarily overwhelmed his senses. As he became used to the flood of sound, it seemed to recede slightly. He realized that the dream up to this point had been completely silent, and the rhythmic pounding was his heart and the raspy buzz was the sound of his breath as he struggled to suck enough air into his lungs to continue to run.

The overwhelming sounds continued to recede as his mind began to understand their source and he was soon able to hear noises not created by his own body. He could now hear the sound of the girls struggling to breathe, and the pounding of their feet on the hard ground.

As he became more able to notice sounds from an ever-widening area, he began to be conscious of a noise unlike any he had ever heard. It was a low growling noise of some large beast. But this was no animal that he had ever encountered. The growling was deep, and steady, as if the creature did not have to pause for a breath. It terrified him to realize that it was gradually getting closer; for he guessed it must be coming from some sort of beast intent on its next meal. And that next meal might just be him. Even though the terror was still coursing through his veins, Micah knew that he must turn and look; he had to know what he would soon be facing.

Slowing down slightly so that he could turn to glance behind him as he ran, his heart skipped a beat when he got a good look at his pursuer. It was huge, white, scary, and unlike anything Micah had ever seen. He did not know what it was, but he knew it sure looked mean.

Suddenly Micah felt himself trip and fall. As he reached out his hands to break his descent, he realized that he was falling into a deep stream, and that he could see the girls had already safely crossed to the other side.

Micah awoke from his dream terrified and confused. It took him several moments to realize he was safely in his own bed. As he wiped the sweat from his face with the sleeve of his pajamas, he wondered why he kept having these strange dreams, night after night. Now that he was awake, he knew that he had never met the girls before, just as he had never in his life seen that field.

How could he have such vivid dreams? This dream in particular had been as real to him as his own bedroom, as real as his foot or his hand. The sweat now on the sleeve of his pajamas proved to him that the feelings he felt were also real.

And how had he scraped his hands? Did he fall out of bed in his sleep and climb back in before he awoke?

What worried Micah most was that the dreams were always about one or more of the same four girls; girls that he was positive he had never seen in his life! As the dreams became more real and vivid, Micah began to wonder if he was receiving a message of some kind. He had never shown any signs in the past of having the gift of dream sight. Was his gift finally developing?

"Father, I had another one of those dreams again," complained Micah early the next morning. "It was about two of those same four girls who wear the funny clothes."

Micah's father, Zebulan, took a drink of the steaming dandelion tea in his cup as he looked up at his son. He glanced at his wife who was busy preparing breakfast, and cleared his throat. She made eye contact with him and gave him a gentle nod.

"Micah," Zebulan began, "your mother and I have been discussing these dreams of yours. We think they might be part of your gift."

He motioned for Micah to take a seat across from him as he continued.

"Son, as you know, no one in our family has the gift of dream sight. Your mother and I have asked everyone we know, all of our friends and relatives, but it is to no avail. None of us know how to train you to best use your talents."

Zebulan paused, and licked his lips nervously. Micah had never before seen his father show any sign of nerves. In fact, Zebulan was known throughout the community for his ability to remain calm in any situation. Why would this talk with Micah cause Zebulan to become so unsettled?

Zebulan continued, "Dream sight is a wonderful gift, if you receive the proper training. But I have heard of many cases where tragedies occurred because a dream was misinterpreted. Because of this, your mother and I have decided to send you to the Royal Academy."

Shock warred with excitement as Micah sat absorbing what his father had just told him. Going to the Royal Academy would be the biggest change of his life, except of course the Rite of Passage. He had never been away from his family for more than one night. The Royal Academy was a boarding school many days travel away. It would mean leaving his friends and family, and making a whole new group of friends. The change could be exciting, but how lonely he would be without his family and away from the home he loved!

Micah could tell by the series of emotions showing on his father's face that Zebulan was unsure whether he really wanted his son to go away to school. Since Micah was the only son, he and his father had formed a very tight bond. But he also understood why his parents were making the difficult decision to send him away to school.

Raising a child in Braumaru was considered to be the greatest of all responsibilities. The parents of a child who grows into a successful and active citizen are honored and considered wise. Conversely, a child who grows into a stupid or lazy adult brings shame to his or her parents. After all, everyone knows it is up to the parents to correct any faults of their children.

Therefore, every parent dreams of and imagines a wonderful future for their child, and plans ways to encourage the child to be as successful as possible.

In Braumaru, one of the best ways to thrive is to learn how to use the gifts with which everyone is born. Natural gifts, just like talents and intelligences, must be cultivated. Most parents feel their responsibility to guide and nurture their children, instilling into their offspring the knowledge that hard work is often necessary to make those gifts work well. A hard working person can increase the power of their gifts, just as a lazy person can let their gifts dwindle away to nothing. It is up to each individual to best use the gifts with which they were born.

Many centuries ago, the people of Micah's culture discovered that there was a direct link between the gift with which a child was born and his or her eye color.

Brown eyed people, like many who live in Braumaru, have the ability to see into the future, which probably explains their fearlessness. They have a strong connection to the earth, and are particularly adept at predicting natural disasters such as earthquakes and volcanoes. This was one reason the people of Braumaru, a group of predominantly brown-eyed people, had the courage to settle virtually at the foot of an active volcano. Without the ability to predict eruptions, not many people would risk living so near the steaming hot lava, even for the beauty of the deep green cliffs overlooking dark blue water and the fertile valley. The land is so rich; no one needs to work overly hard to get what is needed.

Blue-eyed people, of whom there were a few in Braumaru, are able to communicate telepathically. Blue-eyed people can sometimes become so adept at reading minds that they forget to allow the non-telepath to voice their opinion. It can be quite flustering to have your questions answered before they have the chance to leave your mouth. The brown-eyed people of Braumaru have learned to adapt, and have developed the ability to block the unwanted incoming and outgoing messages of their blue-eyed friends.

Most green-eyed people, with their connection to all living creatures and ability to heal, chose to settle in a more inland location. Most of them seem to enjoy wide-open spaces, and become excellent gardeners, animal trainers, and doctors. Because of their special ability with all things that grow, they rarely choose to settle in cities.

Gray-eyed people can most often be found on the open seas. Their special gifts focus most around the weather, both forecasting and controlling. Only the poorest of boats go out to sea without a gray-eye aboard.

Actually, Micah was somewhat of an oddity, and his parents had been unsure how best to help him. He had been born with one blue eye and one brown one.

Seldom in Braumaru are children born with two different color eyes, and everyone in the community was interested to find out if Micah would grow to be somehow different from everyone else.

At 15, Micah still appeared to be just like all of the other young people of his age. But since he had just reached 15, the age at which youngsters' gifts quite often begin to develop, the citizens of Braumaru watched him with speculation.

Wonder of wonders, I have found the knowledge I sought. The Grand Repository, along with all of our records, was spared during the great tragedy. It is very lucky that the building had been built outside the city. Now we can begin to rebuild.

# Chapter 10

ROLAND WAS AGAIN studying the pictures Shanti had taken of the book. Capturing Shanti had been a wonderful stroke of luck. Not only was she a natural at dream travel, but also she was as ignorant of her abilities as a baby. Her parents had really played right into his hands by allowing her to remain unschooled about her natural talents. She had no clue that she had the power to return home on her own.

Roland had discovered her in the dream world, while he was experimenting with the ability to use that form of travel. He was rather good at entering a dream at will, but could not cross over into another realm that he knew existed just out of sight. He had found the door to the other world, but did not have the ability to open it.

While Roland was at the door struggling to turn the handle, it creaked open and Shanti peeked through the doorframe. After a moment of casually perusing his side of the world, she gracefully sauntered through the portal. One look at her eyes had informed Roland that she was a dream traveler. A short conversation had allowed him to discover that Shanti was ignorant about the existence of the two dimensions. To her, she was simply taking a stroll in her dreams.

Even with Shanti holding the door open, Roland had been unable to step through. There seemed to be more to crossing through the portal than just having the ability to open the door. There was still something he lacked.

Roland was smart enough to snatch every opportunity that came his way. There was no telling if he would ever have the good luck to come across another dream traveler from the other world, especially one so lacking in common sense. Imagine, trusting a total stranger, even a dream stranger.

Convincing Shanti to follow him into his world had been absurdly simple. She followed him home like a little lost puppy. Roland guessed that her attitude was understandable. To her, it was just a dream.

Sometimes ignorance really was bliss. At least, Shanti's ignorance was bliss for Roland.

Looking at the pictures Shanti had taken in Professor Jamison's office, Roland once again wished he could chance stealing the actual book. The writing was so faint, he was concerned that he might miss something important. But he knew he could not chance it. His job at the college had been too hard for him to get. He could not do anything stupid that might lose it for him. Being caught sneaking into a professor's office would definitely be classified as stupid.

Still, somewhere in the book there must be a hint that would help him with his plan. It must contain a clue that would tell him how to take that step through the portal into the other world. Roland of Cadal, his great, great, great—who knew how many greats—grandfather, had written the messages. And Roland knew that the first Roland wanted his descendants to travel back home. These messages left in the book must give him the knowledge he was still missing.

The stories that had been handed down through the generations in his family provided most of the information he needed. He knew that his ancestors once had magical powers that they called gifts. These gifts were given by God to a child at birth, and everyone knew the nature of the gifts was usually based on the child's eye color.

Sometime in the past, most of the people of his ancestor's culture had been pushed through a rift into another world of some sort. Those left in this world were mostly uncultured and stupid. Because of this, his ancestor, Roland of Cadal, heir to the throne, had to sweat just like the peasants.

The modern day Roland felt that his family had had a raw deal. He did not want to sweat like a peasant. He wanted to enjoy the life that he deserved by heredity.

Roland wanted to be a king, but instead he was a janitor. A very bitter and unhappy janitor. A janitor with a chip on his shoulder.

Roland had been planning his revenge on the world since his 10th birthday. He had invited everyone in his 4th grade class to his birthday party, but no one had showed up. And this is how they treat someone who should be a king!

Roland had never understood that if you wanted someone to be nice to you, it is often wise to first be nice to them. Having a reputation as the class bully in no way helped Roland become well liked.

But now, Roland had a plan. He would be king...just not in this world. He would be liked and respected.

Throughout his childhood, Roland had listened to and memorized every story about his ancestor. At first, it had been because he was his ancestor's namesake. But then again, every male born into his family was named Roland.

Then, as he got older, he had decided that the tradition of passing down the name and these stories must have a purpose. It must mean that one of those named Roland was destined to rejoin the royal family in the other world, and take his rightful place as ruler.

Roland planned to be that fortunate heir fated to be king.

At first, he had been unsure how to travel to that all elusive other world. Oh sure, the stories had told that it was possible, but not the method. This was very similar to having a truckload of wood dumped in your yard and being told you needed build a house; with no blueprints, and never having laid eyes on a house.

Roland had loved the stories of his ancestors, and had bugged his father to tell them to him again and again. As Roland had approached adulthood, he had discovered something amazing about these stories passed down through his family. Each of the hundreds of stories contained a single clue.

Some of the clues were well hidden, but Roland had long ago memorized each and every story. Discovering the hidden messages of the family legends was simple for a man of Roland's intelligence. One of the clues had led to his discovery of dream travel, and the door. Which in turn had led to the oh-so-fortunate run-in with Shanti.

Soon, he would be where he belonged, with his adoring subjects.

Wait, what was this. Here was a message he had not yet noticed. It was hard to read, but yes, it seemed to be something about borrowing power from someone else.

At last he had found the key. To get through the portal, all he would have to do is find someone from this world with powers and abilities beyond her understanding. She would need to be naïve enough to give Roland her trust, so that Roland could gain control over her fairly easily. A child would be best.

"Perfect," Roland said to himself, "The Eye of Janu has already shown me the perfect child for the job."

There was a fire yesterday. Our Grand
Repository burnt to the ground.
	All of our public records are now lost.
It is almost as if our great civilization had
	never existed. I am afraid that if we don't begin
	to rebuild soon, we will forget all that we once had.
If we forget what we had, who will we become?
	We must start over, rebuild our cities. . .rebuild our
	lives! How can we have a great and mighty culture,
without great and mighty buildings? We need
	our cities for stability. We need someplace where
	we can feel safe and protected.

*Chapter 11*

WITH AS MUCH concentration as Vickie could muster, she kept repeating, "Remember how it was, remember how it was, remember how it was."

Vickie did not know why those particular words popped into her head, or why she was saying the words over and over again. All she really knew was that her friend's brother, Bobby, was being very mean not to let her borrow his skateboard.

The girls often practiced skateboarding stunts on a hill near Tricia's house. Unfortunately, Vickie was not an owner of a skateboard. Every time she wanted to practice with her friends, she was forced to find someone who A) owned a skateboard, B) was not skateboarding, and C) was nice enough to trust her with one of their most prized possessions.

Bobby had fulfilled the first two parts, but she knew she would have trouble with the third. Bobby was a neighbor of Tricia's, the brother of one of Vickie's close friends, an avid skateboarder, and possibly one of the biggest punks in the neighborhood. He practiced being a tough guy at every opportunity, and particularly enjoyed torturing his sister's friends when given the chance. Vickie would usually not even try to get him to loan her a skateboard, but there just wasn't anyone else around she could borrow one from.

It was unfortunate that Laura wasn't part of the skateboarding crowd today. If Laura were skateboarding with the group, Bobby would have to hand over his skateboard. Bobby's parents were strict about him showing good manners towards his sister. But Laura was at the store with her mother, and Bobby was being a royal pain. He had answered Vickie's request for the skateboard with a sneer, an emphatic "NO", and a door slammed in Vickie's face.

That was when the weirdness began.

It was almost as if instinct or intuition had taken over Vickie's actions. She suddenly felt compelled to move out of sight of Bobby's house. A vision of Bobby thrusting the skateboard into her hands became clear in her mind, and she began to chant the words "remember how it was".

This was very strange. The words had no connection to the loan of the skateboard, Vickie, Bobby…or anything, as far as Vickie was aware. But lately, ever since she and her friends had begun looking for things to write about, Vickie had begun to notice all sorts of unusual things. Her eyes seemed to have been opened to a whole new world. It was a rather magical world, that seemed to exist just out of sight. She now realized that she had always caught glimpses of it, shadows or movement where they should not be. But now she was actively looking for these peeps into the other world.

The more she looked, the more she noticed. The more she noticed, the more curious she became. The more curious she became, the more she was willing to open her eyes and thoughts to all that occurred in her own world. It was a shock to discover that even her own world was not the dull mundane place she had once thought.

There was magic all around her. Vickie discovered that she was able to predict things that would happen in the future. She often knew what a person was going to do or say before that person ever had the opportunity to move or open their mouth.

When she talked to her mother about it, her mother said it was called intuition. She explained that instinct was the survival urges that you were born with, and intuition was based on things you had learned. She said that really what happened was that Vickie was very good at noticing things around her, and that her brain did all the processing without any effort from Vickie. That was why she seemed to know what was going to happen before it did, it was her intuition.

All Vickie knew was that her intuition was very strong. Way stronger than that of any of her friends.

Her intuition was now telling her that if she used the chant with enough concentration, she would get what she desired. Or maybe it was instinct. She certainly felt she would not survive without that skateboard.

Suddenly, the door of Bobby's house flew open, and Bobby rushed out the door as if wolves were panting at his heals. He ran over to Vickie and thrust the skateboard into her hands.

"Here, take it!" Bobby yelled. He had a wild, frightened look on his face that Vickie had never before seen. He turned and ran immediately back into his house. The slam of his door echoed in the night air.

"Thanks," whispered Vickie, in shock.

What had just happened here? Had she somehow made Bobby loan her the skateboard?

This was way past intuition or instinct. Had all her practice moving objects with her mind somehow given her the power to make people do as she wished?

"This is scary," whispered Vickie to herself. "But at least I have a skateboard to practice with now!"

With that happy thought, Vickie pushed aside any fears and went to practice stunts with her friends.

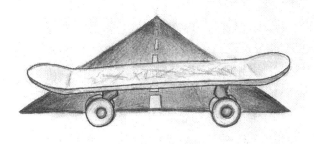

Roland stepped from behind the large oak tree on the corner, and smiled to himself.

This girl was definitely exactly what he had been looking for. She showed promise. She would be very useful to his plan.

Most of those that are left are unlearned and superstitious. After the fire in the Grand Repository, many of them have decided that the tragedy and the fire are a punishment to our culture.

They think our culture angered the great beings, so our society was destroyed.

## Chapter 12

MICAH KNEW HE was just dreaming, but his dreams had been getting progressively realistic. In the way of dreams, he instinctively knew that he was just a bystander. Yet he felt he could reach out and tap the brown haired girl to get her attention.

It did not make sense to try to interact with the people of this dream, and Micah laughed out loud at the ridiculousness of it. Just as he suspected, no one in the room paid the least attention to his outburst of laughter. As in all the other dreams featuring these four girls, he was an outsider.

Still, he wondered what would happen if he tried to touch one of the girls. He had not had the opportunity to be this close to any of them before, and he was curious to know what would happen if he tried to touch a dream creature. Would his hand move through her as if she were made of air? After all, imaginary beings are probably more ghostly than solid. Or maybe, since he was in a part of the dream, it would feel the same as when he tapped his sister on the shoulder. Probably he would just wake up because he had disrupted the dream.

There was only one way to find out. Slowly, with great care, he stretched out his arm and gently placed his hand on the girl's shoulder. "Strange," Micah whispered to himself. "It seems I am not to wake. And by the word, my hand has been stopped, and is not going through her body. So she is not ghostly. But something is different. Her shoulder does not feel as solid as the shoulders of my sisters."

"I can feel warmth, so she feels alive, not like a ghost creature. But it seems to me that my hand is sinking into her shoulder, instead of sitting on top. I do not think I like the way it feels. It is strange."

"I must unravel this riddle. I will take a closer look. Maybe my hand is sinking into her clothing, rather than her flesh."

Taking a deep breath and exhaling slowly, he moved closer to investigate. As he pushed his hand down with a little more force, he exhaled slowly to calm his suddenly racing heart. Was his hand actually sinking into the girl or was it just an optical illusion? Before he could decide, he felt her muscles of her shoulder contract as she flinched away from his hand.

Missy's slumber parties were always fun, but a little scary. Missy lived in an ancient Victorian style house in the old part of town. Most of the girls loved to imagine the many ghosts that must inhabit such an old house. All of the girls were also a little in awe of Missy, because she had the courage to live daily in a house so spooky that the girls often had nightmares about it.

Tricia was just slightly bored as she sat on the couch in Missy's living room. Unlike the other girls, Tricia did not believe in ghosts. To her, Missy's house was just a run-down wreck, with water that never seemed to get hot, and floorboards that groaned with every step. The house compared very unfavorably to her new, modern house, and Tricia hated it that the other girls treated Missy like a queen, just because she lived in a dump. If Tricia could have her way, all slumber parties would be held in her warm, cozy, new home, not in this musty, creaky, drafty, old run-down overgrown shack.

Oh well, thought Tricia, as soon as the other girls realize that there are no ghosts, they'll catch on that this house is not where they want to spend their precious slumber party time. They'll wise up and decide that being comfortable is more important than waiting for nonexistent ghosts to float around the room saying `boo'.

Just as Tricia settled deeper into the cushions, resigned that she must listen to yet another story told by Missy about who had died in her house, and why they are still around, Tricia felt a light pressure on her left shoulder. It felt almost as if someone had laid their hand on her shoulder, which was impossible because all of her friends were in plain view. The pressure on her shoulder really did not scare her at all. It was the sudden warm breeze, almost like someone breathing on her neck, which caused Tricia to squeal and jerk herself closer to her friends.

"Tricia, what is wrong with you," Cathy exclaimed petulantly, "you made me spill my coke. And on my favorite shirt too! Oh, just wait until my mother sees this!"

Cathy had saved her coke from total disaster, but not her shirt. Most of the coke that had been on its way to her mouth when Tricia had jumped was now decorating the front of her favorite white shirt with a Texas-sized stain. Cathy's mother had warned her not to wear it to the slumber party, and now her mother would have the satisfaction of knowing she was right once again. Cathy was more upset that her mother had been proven right about the advisability of wearing the shirt, than she was about the shirt being ruined.

Taking a deep breath to calm herself, Tricia tried to decide if she should tell her friends what she had felt. Were there really ghosts? Had that been a ghostly hand on her shoulder, and a ghostly breath on her neck? Chills raced down her spine as she thought about the possibility of an invisible vampire trying to bite her. Vampires were much scarier than silly old ghosts.

But wait a minute, thought Tricia. If I tell everyone about this, they'll decide it was a ghost, and we'll never have any more slumber parties at my house.

We'll be stuck in this creepy old house every time we want to spend time together. Because one thing is for sure, if ghosts really exist, this creepy old house would have them. I'm keeping my mouth shut about what I felt.

"I'm sorry Cathy, really I am," apologized Tricia, "Something was crawling on me...I think it was a spider."

Karen squealed and pulled her legs up onto the couch, Vickie hunched up her shoulders too keep the spiders away, Missy went to find a jar to capture the spider in, and Cathy shivered. No one could think of anything but the creepy crawly spider on the prowl.

Tricia always had been very good at putting just the right spin on any situation to create a distraction.

Micah sat up in his bed and looked around the dark room. The moon shining through the window allowed him to see that all of his roommates in the dorm were still fast asleep. After rolling over on his side, Micah thought about the dream he had just had.

Had he touched the girl on her shoulder?

Had she really felt his touch?

Our gifts are getting weaker. We no longer are able to devote the time necessary to teach our children how to strengthen their gifts. The schools are gone, families are broken, and all anyone cares about is food and shelter. First our building and people are taken, and then our hope. Without our gifts, we are left with nothing. Something must be done.

# Chapter 13

VICKIE GRABBED TRICIA'S arm.
"What is that? Did you see it? I think I just saw a ghost!" Vickie exclaimed, as she stepped through the door into the spooky old house.

The house, which the girls had discovered just yesterday, had probably been deserted for many years. It was located at the end of a dirt lane, and looked as if it had once been a farmhouse in the middle of the country. The paint on the door was peeling, the lock broken, and the all of the windows were covered with a layer of dirt so thick that light from the sun outside came through more as a haze. The yard, full of weeds and overgrown, resembled a partially tamed jungle. Inside the house a layer of dust like the girls had never seen in their houses covered every surface. The place was ripe for imagination, and exploration.

"Wow, I bet this place is haunted!" Tricia said almost in a whisper. She had done more thinking about what had happened in Missy's house, and decided that ghosts must exist. Why one would bother her she couldn't guess, but she had been spooked ever since. "Do you think we should be here?"

"Sure, no one lives here now," Karen informed her friends. "My parents were talking about this house the other day, and they said that the old man who lived here died, and no one knows where his son lives now. They think it could be a couple of years before the old man's son shows up to claim it. They had a fight years ago, and the son hasn't been around for years. I think I heard that he had moved to another state, or country, or something."

The house was only a block from Karen's house, and it had been her idea to explore it. Karen lived on the outskirts of the subdivision, and the houses on her block had been built long before the subdivision. It was like stepping through a time machine to walk through Karen's neighborhood.

The girls looked around the filthy house. Never had they seen a house so empty of furniture, yet so full of dirt. This was truly uncharted territory. No one had been doing any chores around here for a good long while. Ghosts or no ghosts, this house needed to be explored and cared for! It could become their clubhouse, and no one would be the wiser.

"Look," said Vickie, "my mother will shoot me if I come home all dirty. She'll also ask a lot of questions about where I have been. Let's clean first, and then we can explore."

Micah stood in the middle of the room, watching as the girls happily swept and dusted the old house. The connection he had sensed forming was getting stronger, and he could feel the satisfaction the girls enjoyed as order and cleanliness was restored to the dilapidated house.

With a smile on his face, Micah wandered over to the freshly cleaned window to gaze out into the yard. With a shock, he noticed that the girls were not alone. Hiding behind the shed in the back yard, he spotted the slender figure of a young woman.

Three things were immediately evident to Micah: 1) The young woman spying on the girls. 2) The young woman did not want the girls to know that she was there. And 3) For whatever reason, Micah felt an instant and strong kinship with this young woman.

I finally found some elders with sense. They agreed that in order to survive, we must rebuild. It will not be easy. We only have a fraction of the numbers needed to build a city. We will start small, building just one structure at a time.

# Chapter 14

ROLAND, CLOSED THE notebook with a snap and sighed with satisfaction.

"It is all coming together now," he said with pleasure. "My plan will work perfectly, if I can just succeed in gaining control of that girl."

Roland had just finished reading all the hidden messages he could find in the pictures of the ancient text. It had taken him quite a while to locate the ones he was looking for, but he had finally discovered them. Together, they gave him all the information that he needed. Oh, how great it was to have a compulsive journal writer as an ancestor!

I have searched amongst the survivors, and could find no one with the ability to dream travel. Of all the gifts we have lost, I believe this is one could very well be the saddest. Even though I have never had the ability to travel myself, my training allows me to understand that not all dreams are imagination, some are true dreams. Most importantly, I have had quite a few true dreams lately. My most recent dreams tell me that the missing people are not dead. Somehow, they have been moved from our world into another. I imagine that they must be just as confused about what has transpired as we are. If I could find someone with the gift, maybe I could make contact with my loved ones.

There is no one left with the gift. I am going to try a join. It might be dangerous, joining people with different gifts, but I must try to contact the ones sent into the other world.

Success! I made contact with my father! As I suspected, all those missing have been transported to another world, and are alive and well. Because I was only borrowing power, I was unable to maintain contact for very long. I will try again tomorrow.

*I am filled with much sorrow. The two people who had helped me contact the other world have mysteriously fallen ill. Everyone is afraid they will die. They seem to be blaming me for the illness. I can find no one else who will help me. Everyone is too afraid of the illness to help me try to make contact again.*

Roland now knew what he needed to do, and he had almost all the tools he needed to do it. As soon as he had the girl under his control, he could dream travel to the other world to take his place among the royal family.

No more degrading job as a janitor, cleaning up other people's messes. He would have all the servants he wanted at his beck and call.

No more middle class house with its stuffy closed-in feel. He would have a spacious apartment at the palace, with plenty of windows and bright airy spaces.

No more worrying about bills, or taxes, or how he was going to manage to buy a new car. Others would be paid to assume all his worries and concerns.

But most importantly, he was looking forward to being treated with the all important respect that he deserved.

We had an earthquake
yesterday. The new building
that was almost finished
was destroyed. It does not matter.
We will rebuild.

I have great plans.

# Chapter 15

HER HEART FLUTTERING with excitement, Vickie slowly opened the invitation to enjoy one more look. A hypnotist! How cool! Way better than the baby stuff most people do at birthday parties. And best of all, this was a cousin's party, so none of her friends would be there. If the hypnotist made her squawk like a chicken, nobody important would ever know.

"The Amazing Roland," Vickie whispered to herself with a giggle, "Hypnotist of Kings, and King of Hypnotists."

"How corny," Vickie said aloud, chuckling at the funny choice of words.

"What's corny?" her mother asked as she flipped on her turn signal to make a left turn.

"Oh, I was just looking at the invitation to Sylvia's party. They're having a hypnotist! Do you think I should let myself get hypnotized?"

"Sure darling, why not?"

"Well, it could be dangerous. I heard of a woman who was hypnotized, and from then on, she always barked like a dog whenever anyone clapped their hands. For the rest of her life, she couldn't go to ball games, or plays, it was just too embarrassing. I don't want to go the rest of my life barking or quacking, or making any animal noises."

Vickie's mother smiled at her daughter's silliness. For a girl who so often seemed very mature for her years, her youth often came shining through at the most surprising times.

"Do you really believe that the hypnotist can make you do things you don't want to?"

"Well," answered Vickie with a smile, "I have read some strange stories about hypnotism. And besides, it seems to me that there are a lot of strange things in the world."

"Like what?" questioned her mother gently.

"Well, you know," answered Vickie. "Like the way I see things before they happen. And the times my friends dream the same dreams in the same night. Doesn't that make it seem like telepathy of some sort?"

Vickie's mother took a moment to think before she answered. She wasn't sure exactly what she thought about telepathy. But she truly believed that there was a lot more to the world that she did not know about or understand. After all, her ancestors were known for having a second sight. Maybe her daughter had inherited the gift.

"Telepathy...maybe. But I wouldn't worry about the hypnotist. Do you really think that my sister would let anyone do anything to harm you? You'll be safe at her house. It is her daughter's birthday party. And don't forget, you are my sister's favorite niece."

"Mom, I'm her only niece!"

"Okay then, would my sister let anything bad happen to her only niece? I'm sure that she would much prefer you to stay your own wonderful self, not turn into some animal. I feel confident that she will keep the hypnotist well in hand."

"So, did you enjoy Sylvia's party?"

"Oh Mom, it was great! Roland the Hypnotist really knows his stuff. He promised not to make us do animal sounds, and he said that we would all be as good as new after we were hypnotized. So we all took turns."

"Was it as scary as you thought it would be?"

"No way!"

"Well, spill the beans. What happened?"

"Well, Sylvia tap danced on the coffee table, and you know how shy she is. She must have been hypnotized. All of her friends were made to either dance or sing. It was so cool, and so funny!"

"What about when you were hypnotized, how did it feel?"

"Well, it didn't work for me. I went to sleep like I was supposed to, but Roland the Hypnotist couldn't seem to make me do anything silly like the others. Sylvia said he tried for about 10 minutes before he finally gave up. I guess I'm just one of those people who can't be hypnotized. But it was still cool!"

"So you really didn't have anything to worry about?"

"No, everything was great. I am kind of glad that I couldn't be hypnotized."

"Well, now that the excitement is over, do you want to watch a little TV? Your favorite show is on tonight."

"No, I am so tired," Vickie said with a yawn. "I think I'll go to bed early tonight. I'll tell you more about the party in the morning."

I approached the
elders with my plans. I offered
to lead my people back to greatness.
They refused my leadership. I explained
that as the only surviving member of the
royal family, I am the rightful king.
They laughed.
They said the old way is dead, and
we must find a new way to live.

# Chapter 16

MICAH WAS DREAMING again. He looked around the room, wondering where he was. He knew he had never before been in this room, and he had never before dreamed it. The walls were a pale green, and he could feel the coldness in the air. Turning slowly clockwise, he noticed the blond girl, the one called Vickie, lying on a bed with her eyes closed, breathing shallowly.

"So, it is because of this girl that I am here," Micah said to himself. "By the word, what will happen this time? Will the other 3 girls appear soon?"

Turning towards the door of the room as two people entered, Micah was surprised to see two adults he had never before seen. What was going on here? Why this strange change from his normal dreams? As they began to talk, he decided to listen carefully to their conversation, hoping for clues as to why this dream had a new cast of characters.

"Her vitals are steady Doctor Brown. Do you want me to add any medications to her IV?"

"No, she has only been in this coma for two days. Let's give her a little more time to pull out of it naturally. We have a few more tests to run before we can find out the cause. Where is her mother?"

"I finally convinced her to step downstairs for a bite in the cafeteria. Is there anything you want me to tell her when she gets back?"

"No, just remind her to let us know about anything that she can recall that her daughter might have come in contact with just before she went to bed that night. It could have been something she ate, touched or even smelled. Anything out of the ordinary might give us a clue as to why a child would just go to sleep one night and never wake up."

"Have any of the tests come back positive?"

"No. So far, we have found absolutely nothing physically wrong with the child. She simply went to sleep and drifted into a coma."

I will not let my culture die! As long as I am alive, I will continue to spread the stories of our past greatness. I do not understand how the others can care so little about what we have lost, but I will always care. Some day, I might have a son. My son will know he is descended from kings. He will know of the wonderful gifts we once possessed. I am determined that some day, my descendents will take their rightful place as rulers.

# Chapter 17

ROLAND AWOKE WITH disgust. He should not be awake yet. He needed to still be in the dream state for his plan to work. He must learn to keep himself in the proper state.

The girl must be disrupting his sleep cycle. But ultimately, it would not matter.

It was going to take a surprising amount of concentration to maintain control of both his sleep state and the girl, but he would succeed.

Roland smiled as he thought about how well his plan was progressing. He would learn to overcome his trouble staying asleep.

The girl was already safely tucked away in the house he had constructed in the dream world. It had been laughingly easy to trick her into entering the trap.

And trapped she would remain until he decided she should be released, which would be never.

No, the girl would not be leaving that house anytime soon. While she was in that particular house, he had access to all her natural power.

Oh what a joy it was to feel the power coursing through his body. It made him feel alive, and vibrant, and...yes, all powerful!

Thinking of power reminded Roland of Shanti, the girl he had captured from the other dimension several months ago. It had been amazingly simple to trick her into this world. And the secrets he had learned!

He had figured out right away that she was one of his ancestor's people. He was thrilled to learn about the wonderful gifts his people enjoyed—in the other dimension.

Gifts of power, fantastic gifts that the pitiful people of this world knew nothing about and probably would not believe.

Still, Shanti seemed to be a very nice girl. It was really too bad that he would not be able to let her go free once they traveled back into her world.

Roland had realized very quickly that he absolutely could not travel to the other world without the help of Shanti. She had the power to dream travel, and had grown up in a world where natural powers like hers were recognized and nurtured.

Laughing quietly to himself, Roland reveled in his good fortune. Shanti's family had actually believed that her gift was restricted to telepathy! They didn't even know she could dream travel.

If they had known of her ability to dream travel, her family probably would have provided training, and she would not have been quite so easy to manipulate.

She would not have innocently walked with him into his world.

Still, it was a shame that he would not be able to let her go after they traveled. But he could not take the risk that the people of her world might disapprove of the way he had kidnapped her.

And she might mention the girl he had trapped in the dream house. That would be an absolute disaster.

What to do, what to do?

Wait! Maybe, after she had opened the door into the other world, Shanti could be convinced to enter the dream house. She had such a soft heart. She might enter the house if she believed the hazel-eyed child needed her.

It was so much easier to work with the hazel-eyed child. She knew nothing about dream traveling, nothing about gifts. For her this was one big happy dream. Well, now that she was trapped in the dream house, it probably wasn't so happy.

Shanti, on the other hand, had become much wiser of late. Never again would she innocently follow anyone through any door, even in her dreams. She had learned all too well to be wary of strangers in strange dreams.

Roland closed his eyes and breathed deeply through his nose, preparing his body for the dreams. As usual, the deep breathing calmed his thoughts and allowed him to gently drift off to sleep.

Looking around the light green hospital room, Roland was pleased to see that he had successfully controlled his dream. It had become easy for him to dream travel in this, his own world.

Too bad he needed help to get to the other.

Oh look, he thought, there is the source of my power now. How sweetly she sleeps. I wonder, what will her parents do when she never wakes up? Well, it's not my problem.

As he watched her take another deep breath, he smiled to himself. No one could stop his plans now.

Soon he would combine his own under-developed power with that of the girl, and then Shanti would help him enter the world he knew would welcome him with open arms. The King was going home to his loyal subjects at last.

He began to daydream about the welcome he would receive when he joined his ancestor's people. He could hear the cheering crowd; he could feel the love and respect they would shower on him. He raised his hand to do the royal parade wave, forgetting that it was not very smart to daydream while dream traveling.

"Your help I need," said a voice.

Startled, Roland looked around the room for the source of the voice.

How had he not noticed the teenage boy standing on the other side of the bed? Standing right there, by Roland's source of power?

"Your help I need," the dark-haired boy said again, this time much louder.

Could the boy be talking to him? No, that was impossible. No one should be able to see him while he dream traveled.

Roland looked around the small room, trying to find the person to whom the boy was directing his request. There was no one else in the room.

The boy looked straight at Roland and said insistently, "Sir, aid I need to save this girl. Will you help?"

Shocked that this boy could see him, Roland quickly decided that whoever he was, the boy must be dangerous.

For months Roland had practiced traveling by dreams, and no one had ever paid the slightest attention to his presence.

This was an unexpected state of affairs. The danger must be averted, and quickly.

Roland knew he must take control of the situation, and he knew exactly how he would do it.

"Of course I will help you son, as soon as I find out who you are. Come closer and so I can see you better," Roland commanded.

Micah moved across the room until he stood just a few feet from the strange man who had suddenly appeared, and looked directly into the man's eyes. With a shock, he realized that the man possessed one blue eye and one brown, just like him.

Is this why he could talk to the man? He often tried to talk to people in his dreams, and usually he was ignored. It had given him quite a jolt when the man actually responded to his question.

The man returned the deep look for a minute, then smiled and turned away. Tension seemed to drain from the man, as if he had just put in the last piece of a very hard puzzle. He glanced again at Micah and broke out in laughter.

"You're too late, my dream traveling friend," sneered the man in a menacing tone. "I don't know what your intentions are, but I'm not going to let some youngster interfere with my plans."

Micah looked at the man in confusion. What was the man talking about?

The man looked at Micah's confused face and laughed again. This time, the laughter had a new quality to it, a strange unbalanced note.

Micah had only heard laughter like this one other time, and it made him feel very uncomfortable. There had been an old woman in his village that had lost her sanity, and she had laughed in just such a way.

Micah took a step back, instinctively moving away from the peculiar man. There was a disturbing look in his eyes, as if he did not have full control of his senses.

Somehow, he reminded Micah of a trapped animal. An animal that would stop at nothing to get away; even chew off its own paw, if that was what it took to escape.

But this man evidently did not need to escape, so something else must be making him desperate.

Micah decided he had better be cautious around this man. Who knew what he might do if he felt Micah was a threat.

The man took a step toward the sleeping girl in the bed, and gazed at her with a strange mixture of tenderness and satisfaction. Micah felt a shiver race up his spine. Something was definitely not right here.

"You see in my world, every person is born a powerless baby," the man continued, speaking softly as if to a young child. He reached over to the girl, and gently brushed her bangs off her forehead with his right hand.

Removing the hand quickly from the girl's brow, he jerked his arm up to point angrily at Micah. "In your world," he shouted, "everyone is born with a gift. I plan to go to your world, where I will no longer be powerless."

Micah watched the man's face as the man quite obviously struggled to get control of his fury. Although he could see evidence of many different emotions, anger seemed to be the most dominant. With disgust, Micah realized that self-pity was running a close second.

The man's voice took on the sing-song quality of a storyteller as he continued, "I don't know what your people know about their past, but they were part of this world thousands of years ago. Falling stars hit the city, and it was transported into a new world."

The man looked down dejectedly. "Those of my ancestors who were left in this world were left with nothing. Nothing!"

"They struggled long and hard just to survive," he continued as he made a fist and slammed his right hand into the palm of his left. "I don't know why the gifts were thought so unimportant that there was no time or energy to devote to them. Little by little, those of us left here lost our ability to use them."

"But there is one thing I do know. I don't belong in this pitiful world, I belong in your world," the man continued, turning to look directly into Micah's eyes. "My ancestors were kings, and I am going to rejoin the royal family."

"And if you know what is good for you," he said ominously, "you will stay out of my way."

Micah was confused as much by the man's actions as by what the man was saying. He was at the very least more than a little unstable, and with each word the man uttered, Micah became more and more convinced that the man was at least a bit insane.

It was so confusing! The man seemed to be threatened by Micah's presence, but why? All he wanted to do was help the girl, not interfere with any plans the man might have.

"Sir, I do not know of what you speak, I only know that this girl is in much trouble. By the word, I have been dreaming about her and her friends for the last several months. I feel I know her. Now she is ill and I want simply to help her."

"You have dreamed of this girl" Roland asked Micah, moving a step closer. "Do you know much about dream traveling?"

Micah took another step back as he stuttered an answer. "No...dream travel...no. Mean you...I have heard about dream sight...but...but...I am just beginning to learn about some more rare gifts. There are not many people around who have the ability of dream sight. I am just...just beginning my studies."

"What fools these people are to leave such power untrained. If I were them I would...." began the man, shaking his head in disgust.

Then glancing again at Micah, the man relaxed, and turned suddenly jovial.

"I'm sorry my boy, I think I misjudged you," the man said with a friendly smile. "I hope my early mistrust of you will cause no hard feelings."

He looked around the room as if searching for something and then said, "Good, good, good. Everything looks fine."

"Now boy," the man said with a nod, "why don't you just run along. This girl will be fine, never fear. She just needs to sleep a bit longer. I need to prepare to travel to your world. If you are a good boy, I'll reward you when I rejoin the royal family."

"As a matter of fact, maybe I can reward you now. You've been such a good sport."

Taking out a gold necklace, the man held it up for Micah to see. "Would you like something like this to give to you mother? Take a closer look. See the shiny stone in the center of the gold? Look deeper into the stone. Deep inside there is a special message. Can you see the special message?"

Micah did not know what to think of the man's sudden change of mood, but he decided his best bet would be to humor the strange man. It certainly would not hurt just to look at the necklace.

He took several steps closer to the man, and leaned in slightly so that he could get a good look at the pretty necklace dangling gently in the air.

It was beautiful! His mother probably would like something like a necklace like this.

Would the man really give it to him for her?

Taking one step closer, Micah looked deeper into the center of the stone, trying to find the special message.

It really was a gorgeous stone, so shiny and brilliant. The color was deep and rich, and Micah had a sudden urge to be surrounded by all that pretty color.

He wanted to climb inside the stone, to find out if it did indeed hold a special message.

As the room began to spin, Micah realized too late that the stone was a trap. He felt dizzy, lightheaded, and thoroughly stupid as the room spun faster and he was sucked into the brilliance of the bright red stone.

*What superstitions! Some of the people think that the earthquake came only to shake down our building. They think we should not rebuild. The elders have told me that I should stop talking so much about the past.*

# Chapter 18

RED. EVERYWHERE MICAH looked, all he could see was red. Red swirls, red lights, red fog, even his hands were red. What had happened? Where was the girl who was so often in his dreams? Where had the crazy man gone? Why was he no longer in the room with the green walls? Was this another part of his dream?

It felt too real to be a dream. Fear and uneasiness gripped him, as the nauseating red fog moving around him made him seasick. The red overwhelmed his senses; he could smell and taste something slightly metallic yet slightly sweet like…like…like blood. His stomach roiled with the thought that he might be standing in a great pool of blood.

Micah hoped he had somehow entered into some sort of strange nightmare! At least he had the opportunity to wake from a nightmare.

The swirling red made him dizzy, while the red flashes of light made his head begin to ache. Wherever he was, he wanted to leave as soon as possible.

"Think," Micah reminded himself aloud. "If there is a way into this place—whatever this place is—there must be a way out. All I have to do is look around until I find the way out. I will just take it one step at a time."

Slurp…squish.

"By the word, this is thick. It feels like I am walking through red mud. Much better than blood, though I fear this will take forever."

Slurp…squish…slurp…squish…slurp…squi sh. Micah struggled to take each step, fighting the suction as he pulled his foot out of the red knee-deep mud. How long could he continue to walk, when each step was this much of a strain? Would he eventually place his foot in a wrong spot, and sink so deep into the redness that he could not get out? Would he continue to sink until he could no longer hold his head above the mud, and he would be forced to breathe in its suffocating red thickness?

Micah halted, paralyzed with fear. He was going to die here, surrounded by all this red. His next step might be his last.

Remembering what he had been taught to do in times of stress, Micah took three deep, slow breaths to regain his calm. As he released the first breath, he felt the muscles in his neck relax. The next breath relaxed his back and arms. The final exhalation cleared his head enough that he could once again think clearly.

Looking around, Micah realized that staying here was not an option. He could not stand in this one place indefinitely because he would eventually become too tired to stand. There was nothing to think about. At this point, thinking would only increase his fear. This was the time to act, unless he just wanted to give up.

Micah picked up his right foot and took a step. He would keep moving.

After a few hours, he no longer heard the slurp...squish as he pulled his left foot out of the muck and allowed it to be sucked back down a step ahead of his right. He no longer felt the nightmarish tug as he strained his muscles to once again free his right foot, only to let it sink back into the mud a step in front of his left.

Time became unimportant as Micah stubbornly trudged forward.

"No one in my family is a quitter, and I am not going to be the first. I will find a way out, even if I have to keep walking until my legs no longer will move." Micah said to himself. "I am stronger than any old mud, even gooey red mud...I will not allow it to beat me."

So on continued Micah, step after painful step. Eventually, Micah realized that it had become easier to pull his leg out the mud. Looking down, he became conscious that mud which had been up to his knees, now only covered his ankles. The red fog that had surrounded him was dissipating, and he could see a vague outline, shaped like a house, in the distance.

"Just a few more steps," said Micah to himself. "I will surely be glad to walk on solid ground again." As he stepped out of the gooey red mud, Micah immediately felt energized. It was almost as if he had been struggling through a nightmare, and suddenly awakened. The lethargy and fatigue he had felt for the last few hours, ever since he had entered this strange world of red fog and mud, seemed to fall off him. He now felt light as a feather, and strangely happy. He had not a care in the world.

Free of the red mud, and the fog, Micah took a moment to look around. Behind him he could see the strange red haze he had traveled through, spreading to the horizon like a red sea with no end in sight. Micah's carefree attitude evaporated instantly and he shivered. What a close call he had had. What would have happened if he had begun walking in the other direction? Would he have drowned in a sea of red mud?

"By the word, I do not like this," said Micah, realizing that there might be more danger in this place.

"I do not know where I am, or how I got here. But I think that man had something to do with me being trapped in that mud. I will be more careful; I am not going to easily fall into any more traps!"

Remembering the outline of a house he had spotted in the distance, Micah turned again in that direction.

"Good, it is there still. Houses customarily mean people, and I am tired of talking to myself. I usually like spending time by myself, but it is too quiet and lonely here. It is time to find someone who can explain how I got here, where here is, and how I can get back home."

"Oh, I can help you with that," said a voice directly behind him.

*This world is no longer my world. I do not fit in with these people. I want to rejoin my family, wherever they are. I do not believe they are gone for good, I dream of them all the time. They are somewhere, just out of reach.*

*How can I find them, how can I go on without them?*

# Chapter 19

STARTLED, MICAH TWIRLED around and prepared for the attack he was certain to would follow.

"From where did you come?" Micah shouted, his nerves so taut he could not have whispered if he had tried.

A woman was standing only a few feet away from him, and he knew she had not been standing there only moments before. Since there was nowhere to hide as far as the eye could see, Micah was not only startled, but worried. What was in store for him now? Would this woman send him to trek through a never-ending sea of blue mud?

She looked harmless enough. Her straight brown hair was pulled back into a ponytail low on her neck. She was wearing an ankle length dark blue skirt, low heels, and a light blue sweater. She appeared to be in her early 40s, of medium height, and she had one of those sweet faces that reminded Micah of his favorite aunt. She looked calm, responsible, and rather motherly.

His instincts told him he could trust her…but could he trust his instincts?

"Well," she replied calmly, "you may not believe me if I told you where I came from. Do you know anything about dream travel?"

There was that question again. Another mysterious person was asking if he knew about dream travel.

Of one thing he was certain…he had much need…he absolutely must…he had to find out about dream travel.

Micah took a quick look at her eyes and groaned. Not another one, he thought. I have never seen so many people with eyes mismatched like mine. She probably will ask me to gaze into a blue stone and I will find myself stuck in blue mud.

Swallowing loudly as he mentally pushed away his fears, Micah looked again at the lady. Yes, she had a sweet face like his much loved aunt. More importantly, she appeared to be calm and relaxed, without the fear, self-pity, or anger he had noticed in the man with the red stone. As a matter of fact, she exuded calmness and serenity.

Taking a deep breath to regain his calm, Micah decided to go with his instincts and trust this lady.

"Yes, of dream travel I have heard. But I do not know much. I heard not from my studies, but from a strange man I met," Micah answered.

"Okay, the first thing you must realize is that not everyone can dream travel. A person must be born with the gift."

"Yes, the gift," Micah responded as he thought of the odd man with the red stone. "And could it be that those born with the gift are usually like us, with one blue eye and one brown?"

The woman took one step closer to Micah, and looked intently into his eyes. She had a very serious expression on her face. It looked just like his aunt's expression when she told Micah that his pet cat had drowned in the river. Micah knew that when a sweet-faced person looked this serious, it was best to listen.

"I am not sure about that. I may not have much time, so listen carefully. I found a book that explains a little about dream traveling, and your people. According to the text, there is a special door that is used to go from my world into your world, or your world into mine. Only people with the natural ability to dream travel can open the door and step through."

"Think you that to get out of this place I must find this door? To return home, I must find this door and step through?"

"I think so, yes. Right now you and I are in a dream. When I wake up, I'll find myself comfortable in my own bed. I'll wake like from a normal dream like any normal person. I am not sure how I know, but I am sure that you have gone way past normal dreaming. You have crossed over from normal dreaming to dream traveling. To return home, I suspect that you must find the door."

"How do I find this door? Where shall I look?" questioned Micah as he looked at all the empty space around him. One direction had only the outline of a house dimly seen in the distance, and the other a foggy sea of red mud.

"From what I understand, the door between the worlds is marked by the Eye...." the woman stopped speaking abruptly, and her eyes took on a far away look.

"The eye?" asked Micah. "What mean you by the eye?"

"I must leave now, my alarm clock is ringing. I can feel myself waking up. I'll try to find you the next time I sleep. Good luck!" said the woman, who was quickly fading away.

Then she was gone, and Micah was once again alone.

Turning his back on the sea of red mud, Micah was determined to reach the house. He certainly would not be able to find any door in all this mud; the house would probably have doors aplenty.

Besides, other than his short treks into the woods or times spent fishing, Micah had really very seldom been totally alone. He found that he really did not like it. The quicker he found more people to talk to, the better he would feel. And hopefully, the next people he encountered would not fade away in the middle of a conversation.

It took only a few minutes to cover the distance to the dwelling, which was located on a small hill in the middle of a meadow. As Micah faced the front of the house, he could see that it was a two story building painted sky blue. What surprised him was that it had no windows visible in the front, only one very solid looking door with a huge lock.

"By the word, here is a door, but with a lock. Why would anyone have a lock on the outside of a house? And not just any lock, this lock is bigger than the head on the shoulders of my father. What means this? Is this a trap like the red mud? If I find a way inside, will I be able to get back out? Do I even want to go inside? Could there be people trapped inside, like I was almost trapped in the mud?" Micah asked aloud to himself. Question after question flowed through his head, but no answers.

Deciding that no matter how long he thought through the problem he would not be able to discover an answer to his dilemma, he chose to stop worrying.

"The first thing I should do is discover if there is anyone inside," Micah muttered to himself.

He cupped his hands around his mouth, took in a deep breath, and yelled as loud as he could, "Hello…is anyone in there."

Instead of the expected answering call, Micah's mind was suddenly filled with a vivid picture. The girl he had last seen on the hospital bed was in a room, talking quietly to an older girl. Recognition of the older girl came only after Micah once again felt the strong sense of kinship sweep over him.

Micah had been taught his whole life that whenever he did not know that to do, he should trust his intuition. His intuition told him that the house was indeed a trap, but that it was a trap for the two girls he had pictured in his mind, as well as for him. But trap or not, he knew he had to rescue the girls.

I have made a decision.
I will make an effort to blend in,
but I will never truly become one
of them. I am descended from
generations of kings, and nothing
will ever make me forget that.

# Chapter 20

MICAH TOOK IN a slow deep breath through his nose, held it for a few seconds, and released it equally slowly through his mouth. He repeated this 3 times, as his father had taught him to do. Slowing his breathing would slow his heartbeat, which would in turn help him to keep calm.

Bracing himself for whatever might happen next, he took a step toward the house. With a *whoosh* it disappeared, and in its place was a giant mushroom. Micah halted in his tracks as he looked up at the two story high brown mushroom with purple spots.

"To where did the house go?" Micah muttered to himself. "Houses do not just disappear, and giant mushrooms do not appear. Something odd is going on here, which is not much of a shock. This whole place is very odd."

Deciding to explore around, to see if the house had shifted to another location, Micah turned and took a step away from the mushroom.

Immediately there came again the loud *whooshing* sound.

"I am almost afraid to look to see what is there now," Micah whispered to himself. "There are quite a few things I can think of that are much worse than a giant spotted mushroom."

Taking another slow deep breath, Micah prepared himself for what might now be directly behind him. As he slowly released his breath he turned to see what the mushroom had become.

It was only the house.

Taking a slow step toward the house once again, Micah was really not very surprised to hear the whooshing sound, and discover that the house was now a mushroom.

Deciding that exploration was in order, Micah walked around the mushroom until he had made a complete circle. Something was not right about this mushroom, besides of course its size, color, and ability to appear and disappear with a *whoosh*.

Micah took several steps away from the mushroom. *Whoosh*...now he was standing in front of the house.

Closing his eyes, Micah concentrated on trying to see the two girls he believed were trapped inside the house. The picture he saw of them was reassuring, the older girl was moving around the room, and the younger was sitting quietly on the bed.

"By the word, nothing seems to have changed. Whatever is happening to the house does not seem to be affecting the girls."

Two steps toward the house and *whoosh*...the mushroom was back.

"My father always says that whenever there is something that does not seem like it could be possible, it probably is not. Yet the rules for things here do not seem to be the same rules I am used to at home."

"Might be if I do not look at the house as I approach it, it will not turn into a mushroom. Or it might be that I have to reach the house before it has the chance to change."

Micah moved away from the mushroom several feet, and felt very satisfied to hear the *whoosh* that meant it had once again become a house.

"By the word, if I close my eyes I will not see it change. And if I run towards the house as fast as I can, I may just reach it before it has a chance to become the mushroom. Since I do not know what else to do, I certainly think I have nothing to lose by trying. At worst I will get a few bruises and bumps if I crash into the solid wall of the house."

Moving a few more feet away, Micah assumed a stance that would allow him to take off running at full speed. He was careful to aim himself at the door, which was located dead center in the front. That way, if he veered to the left or the right a little the worst he would do was hit the wall instead of the door.

He would worry about the problem of the giant lock later. He would take one step at a time, even if they were fast running steps.

But now he would focus on reaching that door. The last thing he wanted to do was run right past the house and back towards the tortuous red mud.

"One, two, three, go!" Micah shouted as he closed his eyes and ran as fast as he could toward the house. His heart pounded with anticipation, both for the success in reaching the house, and the fear of crashing into such a hard immovable object.

Running full speed with his eyes closed took more courage than expected.

Just as Micah felt he must have somehow missed the house entirely, he crashed into the solid wood door. At that exact moment he heard the tell-tale whooshing sound. Immediately, the rigid wood of the door disappeared, and Micah's eyes flew open as he felt himself plunging through an opening. He was inside the house!

His moment of triumph turned quickly into fear as the ground beneath his feet ended, and he found himself plummeting over the edge of a high cliff.

I know that this does not seem possible, with everything that has been going on these last years, but I am in love with the most wonderful woman. She is educated like me, and I am fortunate that she was out of the city on that fateful day. She would be the perfect consort for the heir to the throne...if we still had a throne.

# Chapter 21

SCREAMING, "AAAAAAAAH," MICAH plummeted toward the sharp rocks far below. Fear paralyzed both his body and his mind, and he wanted nothing more than to lose consciousness before he slammed into the hard, sharp surface that was fast approaching.

"Fly," whispered a voice in his head.

"If you think you can, you can fly," a stronger voice continued.

"But relax and do not really think...just go UP," the soft voice in his head urged.

Micah did not recognize the voices, but he knew he had nothing to lose by trying the suggestion, and everything to lose by not trying it. He took a deep breath to help release the tension in his body, and pictured what a joy it would be to zoom up into the sky.

Nothing happened, except of course his plummet toward the earth continued.

"This is just a dream, and you can fly if you really believe you can," the soft voice in his head persisted. "You can fly!"

"I can fly...I can fly...I can fly," Micah repeated over and over, trying to convince himself he could do something that he knew good and well he could not. Looking down, he realized he would slam into the ground in only a few seconds. It was too late. He quit struggling to fly, and prepared himself for impact. After all, he did not really believe the old tale that if you died in a dream you died in real life.

Wait...that was it! He was just in a dream, he knew it! Dreams were illogical and wild, and no one could think their way through a dream. Even he, often, did all sorts of unlikely things in them. So why not take off like a bird and fly?

He could fly! He just knew he could.

With that thought, all Micah's fear left him, and he felt all the tension leave his body. Instinctively, he straightened his back a bit and tilted his head toward the sky.

Suddenly, something shifted, and Micah felt lighter than air. He zoomed upward, feeling the wondrous freedom that usually only birds got to feel. He was flying!

What a wonderful experience. Joy filled his heart as he flew over the treetops, the breeze blowing through his hair and tickling his nose. He had never before felt so free, so light and carefree! Of course, he had never before in his life flown like a bird. It felt wonderful to skim the treetops. It felt glorious to be buoyant and weightless!

All his worries about the trapped girls floated away to the clouds as he tried a few flips in the air. They were much easier to do while flying than they were on the ground. It was so much fun to fly; Micah felt that he never wanted to land.

As he flew high in the air, Micah noticed a field of lavender in the distance. Oh, the smell must be wonderful, he thought as he decided to take a closer look. Lavender was his mother's favorite flower. Would not she just love to have a giant bunch for the house?

He flew down closer to the field and landed gently in the middle of the swaying plants. Just as he grabbed the first handful of the fragrant purple flowers, the sound of screams and yells reached his ears. Someone was in trouble!

Professor Jamison yawned as she crawled into bed, still thinking about the lecture she had been planning for the following day. Some of the students were having trouble understanding the importance of context in the archaeological record. She intended to use some modern day examples, if she could just find ones that would interest the students without being too trendy.

As her eyes closed, she realized that she still had not solved the mystery of the boy who had been haunting her dreams. She had been so busy lately, she had almost forgotten about him.

Why did she feel that he was important, and why did she feel she should know him? He was a few years too young to have taken one of her classes, and besides, she certainly remembered everyone she ever met who had one blue and one brown eye. It wasn't common enough to go unnoticed.

Sinking deeper into her pillows, she decided to put the matter of her strange dreams aside. Better to think about the problem of the book, with its strange writing in the margins. Who had written all those messages? Had there really been some sort of meteor shower that wiped out an entire city?

There were some very strange passages in the book. It spoke about certain people having the ability to travel through dreams. And about the city not being decimated, but being pushed into another dimension. Ancient science fiction!

Of course, if she could find proof that any part of the book was true, it would totally shake up the world of archaeology. This area was not supposed to have ever had any cultures complex enough for anything other than a village. The book spoke of huge buildings, and an intricate method of government.

As for those odd beliefs about special gifts and so forth, well, all cultures have their myths and legends.

Using dreams to travel; now wouldn't that be great!

I must go to sleep now, she thought. Tomorrow is going to be a very long day. The worst thing I could do would be to try to tackle it sleep deprived.

As she drifted off to sleep, an image of the boy she had lately dreamed of filled her mind.

In the distance, she spotted a group of children running towards a small village, being chased by the largest brown bears she had ever seen in her life. Her heart pounded as she realized that even if the children reached the safety of the village in time, there will be no real safety. The bears were too huge, and the huts too small.

Suddenly, something swooped down from the sky directly in front of the bears. In shape and size, it appeared to be a person, but it was acting more like a giant gnat.

It swooped and zoomed among the bears, almost as if it was trying to distract the bears from the children. The bears paused in their pursuit long enough to swat at the annoying creature, but the bears were paying as little attention to the flying creature as most people pay to a gnat. They swatted at the creature with their giant paws, and then resumed their course toward the village.

With the illogical suddenness that sometimes occurs in dreams, Professor Jamison found herself standing in the middle of a group of terrified villagers. The bears were on their way, so the villagers were scrambling around, looking for a safe place to hide themselves and their children from the ferocious beasts.

But Professor Jamison knew that no matter how hard the children tried to hide from the bears, it would be impossible. One look at the frightened children was all it took to figure out what had happened. The village children had raided a honey tree, and they were covered with the sticky goop.

The smell of honey filled the air, and the entire village was perfumed with a bear's favorite fragrance. The bears' noses would unfailingly lead them directly to the offending children. Particularly since each child was so covered in honey they smelled like a giant honey lollipop.

Professor Jamison watched in horror as a growling mass of angry fur broke through the trees that surrounded the village. Its growls seemed to echo in the open area surrounded by the villagers' huts. The bear stopped in the middle of the village square and stood up on its hind legs, lifting its snout into the air and then letting out a tremendous roar.

It must be at least 8 feet tall, thought the professor. How are the villagers ever going to be able to protect themselves against a beast this size?

The bear took a few more sniffs in the air, and dropped down onto all fours to head toward one of the huts. Professor Jamison remembered two of the children running into that hut to hide, and she desperately looked around for something, anything, that she could use to distract the furious bear from the helpless children. She noticed a walking cane leaning against the side of one of the huts and had just started to move toward it when her heart fell into her stomach.

Storming into the village square were four more mountains of muscle and teeth, all in a towering rage.

Suddenly, something zoomed out of the sky, and landed with a loud thud on the roof of the hut that the first bear had chosen to explore. The bear, that was just about to stick its head into the dark interior of the hut, changed its mind and stood on its hind legs to investigate the noise. Professor Jamison shielded her eyes from the sun. She recognized the new arrival as the human gnat she had seen before. She wanted to get a better glimpse of the strange flying creature.

No! It couldn't be!

The human gnat was the boy who had been lately starring in her dreams. The boy she did not know, but who she felt she should know.

Without ever meeting him, she instantly knew his name was Micah.

Who was this boy? How did he fly? Could he help the villagers escape from the bears? Why was he invading her dreams?

Professor Jamison watched in awe as Micah tilted the bucket he held in his hand just enough to spill a cupful of thick, rich, honey directly onto the bear's nose. The bear immediately dropped down onto all four legs in confusion. It scraped at the honey covering its nose, and its large rough tongue began the long, but satisfying process of removing the sticky treat from its face.

Micah flittered around the bears like the honey fairy, depositing a cupful of the sweet fragrant honey on each bear's nose. Each bear had the same response as the first bear. It immediately forgot its anger, and began the process of consuming its favorite sweet ambrosia.

Of course, thought the professor. The plan was really simple, yet brilliant. The bears wanted honey, and would follow the scent until they found their treat. Give them what wanted and they would be happy. Fill their noses with honey, and they would be unable to sniff out the honey-covered children. What a creative way to help the villagers!

Professor Jamison watched as Micah gave each bear a dose of the calming honey. She wondered what he would do next. He had certainly calmed the bears' rage, but now they looked suspiciously like they were ready to lay down in the village square for a prolonged nap.

The villagers would not be safe until the bears were back in their own territory, and far away from the small community.

Micah once again began his human gnat routine, flying close enough to irritate the bears, but high enough to be just out of reach of their sharp powerful claws. When he had gotten their attention, he flew to the edge of the village and deposited a cupful of honey on the ground.

The bears, realizing that there was more of the treat to be had, followed and immediately devoured the delicacy. Micah moved deeper into the forest, further away from the village with his bucket of honey, and the bears followed like trained dogs waiting for their treat. In this way, Micah lured the bears away from the village, with Professor Jamison watching and following. When he had the bears several miles from the still terrified villagers, he deposited the bucket of honey in the lowest branch of a tree. Micah left the bears to their honey, and flew away.

Professor Jamison awoke with a gasp. She was sitting up in her bed, and the numbers on the clock read 3:23 am.

What a crazy dream, she thought.

She lay down on her bed, and took a deep breath to help relax back into slumber.

That's strange, she thought to herself as she drifted off to sleep, I could almost swear that I smell honey.

Micah found a good landing place in the field, the long stems of the purple flowers gently waving in the breeze. Realization of what this all meant hit him as his feet gently touched down onto solid ground. He was able to fly because he was in a dream.

That meant the house that changed into a mushroom was not real, the red mud was not real, the cliff was not real, and the field in which he was now standing was not real. There was nothing here that could really harm him, unless he let it. Dreams are made up of imagination, are they not? Should not he be able to control what happens around him?

He did not need to be afraid of anything. Except...what about the woman and two girls? He had seen the woman observing in the village, but he had ignored her because he had noticed that neither the bears nor the villagers had taken any notice of her. Was she a part of the dream, or real? And were the two girls who he believed to be trapped in the house a figment of his imagination, or real?

"We are most certainly real," the soft voice in his head whispered. "And we want you to help us escape from this horrible house."

Life is good. I know this.
Food is plentiful, the weather is mild as
always, I have a wonderful wife and even
a few friends. Yet I cannot forget how it is
supposed to be. I feel that my
destiny has been snatched away
from me by the tragic events that
happened years ago. What would my
life have been like if I had become king
as I had been destined to do?

# Chapter 22

WITHOUT EVEN REALIZING it, Micah spoke out loud to himself. "How to return to the mushroom house? I do not even know if I should go north, south, east, or west from this place...or if there even is a north, south, east, and west in this crazy land of dreaming."

"By the word, let me think this through. In dreams, you must often just let things happen. Might be, if I take off flying and picture the house in my head, I shall go the right way."

Using his newly acquired skill of flight, Micah rose in the air about 200 feet. Slowly flying in a small circle, he carefully looked in all directions for any sign of the mushroom house. Nothing of the house could be seen.

He tried picturing the house in his mind, but could not. The thrill of flight was too distracting. Deciding that he would be better able to concentrate if he was unable to see how high he was, he flipped over onto his back, closed his eyes, and decided to trust his intuition. He did not want to fly blind like this; it was just as scary as running blindly toward a solid object. But in a dream world, intuition seemed to be a better guiding force than logic.

Following his intuition was not one of Micah's strengths. He tended to think that if he just thought about something long enough, he would find a better way to do something, an improved location to put something, a superior way to say something. He usually spent so much time thinking about what he was going to do that he rarely got around to doing it.

After flying blind for a few minutes, Micah decided to flip over and take a peek at the ground. This flying without seeing was nerve-racking!

There it was! Almost right below him! Another minute and he would be directly over the mushroom house's roof.

What a way to travel. No walking, running, or riding. No need for maps, signs, or roads. He just let intuition take over, and he arrived at his destination. No worry, no tiredness. This was great!

In the distance behind the house, Micah spotted the dreaded lake of red slime.

"I must need to get rid of that horror," Micah muttered. "I will just close my eyes again, and think it away."

Because he did not want to take the risk that he would float off to another location, Micah landed a few feet away from the front of the house. Closing his eyes, he imagined the house, surrounded by green fields…and no red slime. When he felt he had concentrated as much as he could, he opened his eyes to see the result.

"By the word, it is still there!" Micah mumbled to himself. He did not know what it was about the red slime that frightened him so much, he just knew that he would be very happy if it disappeared and he never had to see it again.

"Well, I must remember about this," he muttered. "Just wishing something gone does not mean it will disappear. I guess the slime is here to stay."

"Now it is time to get down to business. I am here at the mushroom house, and I need to figure out how to get the two girls out of that house."

Micah concentrated on the girls, willing them to communicate with him again. Up to this point, they had started any mental conversation.

They had told him that they were trapped in the mushroom house. Put there by a man that he suspected was the same strange man in the hospital that had somehow transported him here. And he felt compelled to help them get out. He could no more leave them trapped in the mushroom house than he could leave his younger sisters on a rock with the tide coming in.

He simply did not know how. This business of trusting your intuition instead of thinking things through was strange indeed.

Concentrating on his mental picture of the girls, he tried to imagine himself in the room with them. Nothing happened.

"By the word, this really is just like a dream," Micah muttered. "Much control over what happens is not in my hands. I will have to try from a different location; like maybe the roof. Maybe having height will help."

Flying was now easy for Micah, and he enjoyed the weightless feel as the wind rushed through his hair. Why, flying up to the roof of the mushroom house was not going to be any harder than jumping over a mud puddle.

Just as Micah's feet were about to touch down on the mushroom cap shaped roof of the house, something came hurtling out of a cloud, barely missing Micah and throwing him off balance. He instinctively reached out to catch himself, and found that he had grabbed hold of a very strange—

but quickly moving—flying contraption being driven by 3 kids.

"I told you it wouldn't work! Now we are in bigger mess than before!" shouted the red haired girl directly in front of Micah. None of the 3 flyers seem to have noticed that they had acquired a new passenger.

As Micah struggled to pull himself into the swiftly moving flying machine, he realized that it was really just a rowboat with wings. The open design made it easy for him to pull himself into the contraption, and the fact that all three of the youngsters were huddled over some sort of instrument at the front of the 8 foot boat gave him plenty of opportunity to look around.

"Strange," thought Micah out loud to himself. "What is making this thing fly?"

"Watch out, it's coming after us again," shouted the blond boy closest to the dark haired girl who was steering the vehicle.

Within seconds, a horrific screech heralded the entrance from the clouds of two strange, translucent, dragon-like creatures. Micah had never seen anything like the creatures, and hoped never to see them again.

The creatures were rather ghostly looking, having see-through, milky white bodies with only the slightest tint of split-pea-soup green. Their heads and wings were of a darker green, but still translucent.

The most disturbing thing about the creatures was that the lower halves of their bodies were missing. It was almost as if the creatures had been climbing through a window, and their lower halves were stuck outside while their upper halves were inside. The effect was disconcerting to say the least. It was not possible for half-creatures to fly through the sky, yet there they were.

Fear coursed through Micah's veins. What were these creatures, and why were they chasing these kids?

He must help.

"Head for the roof of the house below," shouted Micah.

Three stunned faces turned in Micah's direction.

"Who...who are you? How did you get on our boat?" shouted the boy.

"An explanation I will give later. These creatures, I fear they must be very dangerous. To get away from them, aim straight for the roof of the house, and hold on."

"We'll crash."

"Trust me," yelled Micah. "Quickly, they have begun to gain on us!"

I now have a son! It is the proudest day of my life, and the saddest. My father had a kingdom to give me, but I have nothing to leave my son. How can I teach him our proud family traditions, when all of the family is gone? Will my little Roland grow up knowing only the wildness of this place?

Can I teach him and make him understand the significance of his heritage?

# Chapter 23

THE RED HAIRED girl looked courageously at her fellow shipmates.

"Let's do it!" she yelled. "I'm not as afraid of crashing into a house as I am being caught by those creatures. You know what they did to the monster from our lake!"

With a nod of her head, the girl driving the flying contraption aimed straight down. "Hang on everybody, we'll hit in about 20 seconds!"

Micah, having second thoughts about the advisability of crashing into the mushroom house, looked once again at the strange creatures speeding towards them. One glance at their razor sharp teeth, and he knew this was the right decision. Or at least, he hoped it was. Surely they would go through the roof just as he had gone through the door.

"10 more seconds!" yelled the blond girl.

Micah suddenly remembered that the last time, he had had his eyes closed.

"Close your eyes!" Micah yelled.

"What, are you nuts?" shouted the boy. "We couldn't see where we are going!"

"Trust me, and close your eyes!"

The kids looked at each other, and silently decided to trust their new passenger. They closed their eyes. With only 5 seconds until impact, they would soon know if their trust was misplaced.

Of course in 5 seconds it would be too late change their decision. It was probably too late already.

*Whoosh.*

As soon as Micah heard the *whoosh*, he knew that he had made the right choice. They were through the roof of the mushroom house.

"We're through! We didn't crash," cheered the pilot of the flying boat.

She pulled back on the steering wheel, so that the boat leveled off and no longer aimed toward the ground.

"But where are we?" questioned the boy.

Micah recognized the place. It was the same cliff he had fallen over when he first entered the mushroom house. Only now, since he was not plummeting toward his death, he had time to notice the openings in the side of the cliff. The cliff wall was littered with caves of all sizes.

The two girls he had seen in his mind must be in one of those caves.

Looking at the cliff wall, Micah noticed one small segment that did not have any caves. He was surprised that he felt compelled to go toward that segment.

Once again he was faced with intuition versus logic. Logic told him the girls could not be where there were no visible caves; intuition told him that this was the place where the girls were trapped.

But before he could help the girls, he needed to help these children. He had always been taught to protect those younger and weaker than himself.

"Let us land this flying contraption," Micah suggested. "I must continue on my way, but desire first to hear your story."

After they had landed, Micah took the precaution of leading the children into a nearby cave. Could those creatures follow them into the mushroom house? Micah did not know, but wanted to feel a modicum of safety as he listened, fascinated, to the story the children had to tell.

It seemed that the kids had wished those ferocious creatures into being. They had wanted the creatures to get rid of a monster that lived in the lake by their houses. The monster terrorized their village and had eaten many of their pets.

At first, all was well. The creatures quickly devoured the offending lake monster, and the children rejoiced that their pets would now be safe.

Until, the newly created creatures proved to be much more dangerous than the lake monster. They turned their sights on the children. As a matter of fact, they began to terrorize the entire village.

The kids did not even know how they had created the creatures, much less how to get rid of them.

No one in the village had been hurt yet, but only because they had immediately moved into concealment. The villagers were now hiding out in their underground storage areas, which thankfully were full of food. Unfortunately, they were not full of water and someone had to periodically face the creatures to get water.

The children had finally decided that since they had created the problem, it was up to them to fix it. They had snuck out of their bunkers early in the morning, and had spent the last few hours trying to draw the creatures away from the village.

Only...they had not thought the plan through. They had no clue where they should draw the creatures away to, or how they would get back home without the creatures following them back.

The kids had been racing around for hours, and were exhausted and frantic. It seemed that no matter how fast they flew, they could not lose the creatures. They had been on their third pass past the house when they had accidentally acquired Micah as a passenger.

*Whoosh*. The dragon-like creatures suddenly appeared in the sky. With a loud screech, they began circling, and appeared to be searching for the children.

What a strange sight they were, with their two front feet, two wings, pointy nose, and no back half. Even though they appeared to be only half creatures, they look ferocious beyond measure. Micah wondered if they were cranky because they were stuck halfway between two worlds.

An idea suddenly took hold of Micah's imagination and ran away with it. If he went back with the children to their village, he might be able to help them discover how they brought the creatures here in the first place. If they could discover how they got here, it should be possible to discover how to send them back again.

It was getting pretty obvious—with the way the creatures followed the children without rest—

that they had a personal vendetta against the youngsters. The only hope the children had of returning to normal life would be if the creatures were returned to their own world.

"I will try to help you get back to your village. Can you describe to me its location?" Micah asked.

The boy looked out of the cave at the dragon creatures swooping around and screeching. This person wanted to go back out there where the creatures were?

"You know, I think I'll stay right here for a while," the boy said with finality. "I really don't feel up to taking on those two right now." He pointed toward the mouth of the cave and grimaced.

"We can only stay in this cave a short amount of time. Eventually, we will all get hungry and thirsty. By the word, I think I can help you get rid of the creatures for good," Micah explained. "But we need to go back to your village. I might be able to get us there without going past the creatures, but I first need to know more about the location of your village. Please, can you describe the village to me?"

"It is the small settlement that is next to the lake, between the two mountains, in the forest of evergreens," the boy eagerly said. He was imagining a method of travel where the four of them were instantly transported from the interior of this cave straight to the warm safety of his family's storage center. No need to deal with the dragon creatures at all.

"There are no evergreens, or mountains," scoffed the blond girl. "Those are palm trees. Haven't you paid any attention to the trees you have lived around your whole life?"

"Palm trees, evergreens! What are you two saying? We live next to a lake in the middle of the desert! There are no trees at all." said the red haired girl.

Suddenly, Micah felt a change in the air. It was almost as if the air itself stopped all movement, and the earth suddenly stood still.

The blond girl, with a far-away look in her eyes, muttered "Just five more minutes please?"

Then she faded away.

The boy jerked, as if startled, and faded away.

The red haired girl said with a sigh of relief, "Oh, it's only a dream."

Then she also faded away.

Micah moved to the mouth of the cave, and cautiously looked outside. Not only were the creatures no longer screeching high in the air, they were nowhere in sight. The flying boat was also gone.

I caught little Roland playing with some of the peasant children today. It must stop. He must be made to understand that he is not like those other children. While they come from peasant stock, he is of royal blood. I must make him understand. I must protect my bloodline, so that my descendants will be able to rule. I must.

# Chapter 24

MICAH LOOKED AROUND him stunned.

"This was all a dream shared by those three, and I was a part of it?" Micah softly asked. He knew there was no one near to hear him speak, but hearing any voice, even his own, was reassuring.

"And here I am, left alone again. I never before knew how much I enjoyed the company of others," he said with a sigh.

"By the word, is this whole thing a huge, peculiar dream? And what of the two girls who keep speaking in my head. Are they also going to disappear right before my eyes, and leave me wandering all alone in this place of strangeness?"

Micah looked again into the cave where the children had been, and then out at the sky that had lately been populated with the ferocious dragon creatures. He thought a moment about his recent experiences, and shook his head.

"But no, I can feel a difference. Those three children were strangers to me, I felt no kinship, no sense of knowing. The girls from my head have a connection to me. I must continue to look for them. Maybe together we can escape from this confusing dream world."

"Of this I am sure; this is not simply one of my dreams. As real as my dreams have lately become, this is far more real. I will do as my father taught me and follow my intuition. My intuition tells me to escape, but first I must find the two girls."

Leaving the cave, Micah looked up at the face of the cliff. It was virtually littered with caves. It would take him years to search all of those caves, and Micah did not feel he could live all alone in this strange place for years.

This was even worse than waiting for his birth gift to show itself. At least at home, he knew the rules, and knew what to expect around each bend in the road. He might not yet know the form his birth gift would take, but he knew vaguely what to expect. As a brown-eye, he should be able to foresee the future. As a blue-eye, he ought to be able to communicate telepathically. Since he had one blue and one brown eye, his birth gift might not be as predictable as usual, but it must be related to one of the two.

Here, there were no rules that he could determine. Every time he felt he had something figured out, he was proven wrong. Entering the mushroom house was not as simple as going through the door. He could not think away the sea of red goop. The three children and the dragon creatures just disappeared.

How had he helped the villagers who were being attacked by bears? Were the villagers actually dreamers who were enjoying a deep slumber? Were they a part of a dream he was having? Were they somehow real?

"Micah, where are you?" the soft voice in his head broke into his thoughts. "We are getting weaker, and we need your help."

"Where are you?" Micah yelled. All the frustration he had recently felt, coupled with the questions rolling around in his head, caused his patience to be very near its end.

"We are trapped in the house. Please come find us."

"There is no house in sight. I cannot find you!" Micah shouted as he turned in all directions to look for a house. Micah noticed that the voice did indeed sound weaker, and it scared him.

"We will concentrate all of our thoughts on you. I'm afraid that is all the help we can give you," broke in the stronger voice. The voice that he knew belonged to the older girl, the one for which he felt so much kinship.

Almost instantly, a picture entered Micah's mind, and shoved all other thoughts aside. The vision was so strong that Micah was unable to focus on anything else. Now, all he could see were the two girls in a dark room. He could only dimly see the cliff face that he knew was directly in front of him.

Allowing intuition to take over once again, Micah flew. As he rose into the air, the picture in his mind continued to become clearer and clearer. It was as if the closer he got to the girls, the better they could communicate.

Beyond the vision of the girls, he could see the fuzzy cliff face. He was being drawn to the only spot on the cliff face that appeared to have no caves! What a great place to hide an entrance you did not want anyone to find. No matter how long someone searched the caves, no one would search a blank rock face.

His ascension finally halted, and he felt his body just naturally move into a prone position. It was very strange letting his body move without conscious thought. He fought the impulse to regain control and concentrated on relaxing.

Perhaps the scariest thing of all was that he had little doubt that he was going to fly directly into the cliff face.

A solid cliff made of hard, hard stone.

Could he do it, could he let himself slam into the side of a cliff?

What if this cliff was not like the mushroom house? There might be no magical *whoosh*, there might be no mysterious transformation that allowed him to move through solid objects.

"Okay, the best that could happen is that I will find myself through the cliff wall and in the room where the girls are trapped. The worst would be that I will hit solid stone with my head."

That would hurt.

By the word, that would hurt a lot!

Micah retook control of his body just long enough to roll over on his back and close his eyes. At least he did not have to see himself speeding toward what might be his doom.

*Whoosh.*

Startled by the sound, Micah's eyes flew open and he halted his flight. About two inches above his nose was a ceiling. He was through! Not only did he not slam into that cold, hard cliff face, but he had made it through!

Landing softly on the floor that was located just a few feet below him, he noticed that it was indeed a finished floor, and not dirt or stone. He was definitely in a house, and it must be the same house where the girls were trapped.

Taking a moment to acclimate himself to his surroundings, he realized that he no longer could see the picture of the two girls in the dark room. What did that mean?

Micah took three deep breaths to regain his calm, and moved toward the only door in sight. As he touched the door handle, a feeling of success shot through his body. The girls were in the next room, he was absolutely certain.

Roland is growing into a fine young man, and one who fully understands the need to keep himself away from the unworthy that surround us. We have arranged a marriage for him with the daughter of one of the few noble families left. The nobles have recently begun to gather together. We have a plan to join our scattered resources and create a sovereign kingdom once again.

# Chapter 25

THE GIRL SHOUTED, "Micah," as the door swung open. She sprang up from where she had been sitting cross-legged on the floor and rushed over to welcome the bemused looking boy.

"Micah, I am so glad you are finally here. Shanti and I hope that you can help us get out of here. Oh, and my name is Vickie."

The girl reached out and grabbed Micah's arm and pulled him fully into the room. Her hand burned on his arm, but a smile lit up her face. Micah was reassured to see her up and active, rather than lying still in a hospital bed. Helping this girl was the right thing to do.

The teenage girl sitting quietly in a chair gracefully rose to her feet and approached Micah.

She waited until Vickie finished her bubbly introduction, and clasped Micah's elbows in such a way that their forearms met. It was the traditional greeting of welcome of Braumaru. And it made Micah feel instantly at ease. This girl also deserved his help.

"We have explored this house from top to bottom, but can find no way out," Shanti explained to Micah. "There are no windows; doors which open onto solid walls; and hallways that only lead to dead ends. Yet by the word, if you can find a way in, we must be able to find a way out."

"I spent much time with the man called Roland," Shanti continued, "and I know much of his plan. He spoke of traveling through dreams from one world to another. To do this, he needed the help of others."

Shanti turned away from Micah and hung her head as she continued, "To my shame, I have helped him. It was with my help that he brought Vickie here to the land of dreams, and I helped him open a door which allowed him to travel to another world."

"He said that it was to my world he goes. He said that it was the world to which he really belonged. I have helped him, because I needed his help to get back home. Yet I could not follow. I could not leave Vickie trapped in this world of dreams."

Turning to look Micah straight in the eyes, she pulled herself up straight. "I need your help, we need your help. I cannot find the door Roland used, that would allow us to go home. Help us find the door, please. I have noticed that the longer we stay here, the weaker Vickie becomes. We need to get her out of here before she becomes too weak to walk."

Looking at the girl named Vickie, Micah felt a sudden pity. How long had she been trapped in this strange land? Looking more closely, he noticed that she had dark circles under her eyes, and her motions were jerky and jittery. He reached out and touched her forehead, only to realize that she was burned with fever.

"I have been traveling around this world of dreams, and I have learned that to find something, you cannot look for it," Micah explained to Shanti.

"What we must do is concentrate on what we wish to find, and just let our intuition take over. We cannot make ourselves find the door, we must simply let ourselves find the door," Micah continued.

Shanti sighed in relief as she realized Micah meant to help. "If we concentrate together, like Vickie and I did to help bring you here, I think we will be stronger. But let me warn you, Vickie is now so sick, I do not know if she will be able to concentrate for very long."

"Let us try," said Micah, as he clasped Shanti's arm. Shanti clasped Vickie's and Micah completed the circle by grabbing Vickie's other arm.

Micah closed his eyes, and thought of a door to his world. His mind kept switching to doors of different shapes and colors...he just did not know what the door should look like.

Unexpectedly, he remembered the woman he had met just outside of the sea of red goop. She had mentioned a door with an eye on it. Micah visualized a door with the ancient symbol of the Eye of Janu, a symbol he had seen at various sacred sites his entire life.

"Oh look, it's that eye that was over my bed," shouted Vickie with excitement, as she jerked her hands away from Shanti and Micah and broke the circle.

Micah and Shanti opened their eyes and turned to look in the direction Vickie was now pointing. On the same door Micah had recently entered the Eye of Janu was now visible.

Could this be the door they should go through to get home?

Shanti, recognizing the door as the one leading to her world, slowly smiled. Micah looked at the relief on Shanti's face. Shanti and Micah looked at each other, and slowly nodded their heads. There was no need to talk, both understood that they had to give it a try.

Shanti and Micah both took several deep breaths to prepare themselves for whatever they might find on the other side of the door. Would they reenter their own world, or find themselves in a place even stranger than this one? Was this a trap, or the way out?

Micah gently grabbed Vickie's left arm and Shanti her right. Vickie was too weak to go through the doorway on her own. Shanti reached out and opened the door, so far so good.

Micah moved forward to peer through the door, and was unnerved to discover that nothing could be seen but darkness. This was not going to be easy. There was no clue to what might lie on the other side. There might be monsters, red goop, or maybe absolutely nothing.

As he took a deep breath to brace himself, Micah stepped through the doorway and pulled Vickie and Shanti behind him.

Looking around him, Micah was pleased to find that he was standing in the reception room of his school dormitory.

"We did it!" Micah yelled.

"We are not trapped any longer, we are back in our own world!" Shanti exclaimed excitedly.

"So we're safe now?" Vickie asked with a smile, and then collapsed unconscious into a heap on the floor.

My people have gone crazy.
They are burning anything they can
find that reminds them of our old
way of life.
They say they will not allow us to set
up our government again the old
way, and that they do not want a
king. I will not give up, but I must
become more secretive. I will hide
this book in a safe place, since my
entries could be used against me.

# Chapter 26

THE ALARM SOUNDED urgently, startling the nurse out of her reverie.

"The heart monitor on the girl in room 213 has just gone flat. Get a doctor to the room now!"

The nurse rushed down the hallway, hoping that the monitor had somehow come unplugged, but truly expecting the worst. The young girl's case was just too much of a mystery to know what to expect. Expecting the worst prepared you for the shock of losing someone so young, someone that appeared to be perfectly healthy—except for the unexplained coma.

The nurse entered the room, but froze just inside the doorway, blocking the entrance. The doctor, only a fraction of a minute behind her, shoved her aside and raced over to the bed…the empty bed.

Moving slowly because of her state of shock, the nurse inched forward to stand by the doctor, her face showing a mixture of confusion and concern.

"Doctor, how are we going to explain to this girl's parents that she just disappeared, into thin air?" Nurse Johnson whispered to the doctor, her brow creased with worry.

"Don't be ridiculous," Doctor Brown reprimanded gruffly, "She evidently awoke from her coma confused, and is now wandering around the hospital somewhere. We'll find her quick enough."

"No we won't, Doctor. She's not wandering around, she disappeared."

"Nonsense," huffed the doctor. "I have seen numerous cases where a comatose patient awoke, and then began to wander around in confusion."

"You don't understand," Nurse Johnson looked the doctor directly in his eyes, making sure that his attention was fully on what she was about to say. "I had just checked on her. I had checked to make sure the machines taking her vital signs were working properly. Back at my station, I could hear the beeps that measured her heart rate as I looked at her room."

"You see, I have a daughter about her age, and I was thinking just how devastating something like this would be to my family. I was gazing at her room, feeling sorry for her family, wondering if she would ever wake up."

"So I almost jumped a mile when the alarm sounded to warn that her vital signs had stopped. I didn't even turn to look at the screen. I just rushed to her door, yelling over my shoulder for someone to call a doctor."

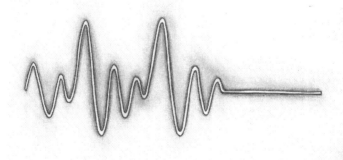

Doctor Brown, began to look concerned, but was still not convinced. "Stay calm Nurse, we'll find her. You must have looked away just long enough for her to slip out of her room. It is just one of those strange coincidences."

"No doctor," Nurse Johnson continued with a hopeless sound in her voice. "From the time her vital signs went flat, I never for a second took my eyes from her door. And there is no other way out. She disappeared into thin air!"

"People don't disappear into thin air," the doctor said forcefully.

"Well, this girl did!"

"I think she awakens," whispered a voice as Vickie began to gain consciousness.

Vickie didn't know where the voice came from, but she did know that she could not open her eyes while the bright light of the sun shone so intensely through her eyelids. It was brilliant enough that she just knew that if she opened her eyes before they were ready, she would be blinded for life. Best not risk it.

Besides, she had that groggy feeling she sometimes got when she had been asleep for too long. It would feel much better to prolong the moment when she would really have to wake up.

Yawning, she stretched out her arms over her head.

Pop...pop...pop...pop...pop...pop...pop...p op... pop...pop...pop.

"Wow," Vickie mumbled through another yawn, "That sounded like popcorn popping."

She began to sit up, but paused to continue her one-sided conversation with herself. "Oh…I ache all over. I must have slept way longer than usual!"

She heard a shuffling noise nearby and mentally groaned as she thought of what that shuffling noise probably meant. It was either her little brother sneaking into her room to snatch one of her belongings, or it was her mother coming to tell her she was late for breakfast.

Either way, it was time to face the day. Vickie gingerly opened her left eye so that she could see whether she needed to jump up and rush around getting ready for school, or if she needed to exercise her vocal cords as she yelled at her brother. Her other eye immediately flew open, and then half-way shut again because of the glare, and she gasped in surprise as she jerked up to a full sitting position.

"Hey, where am I?" she squeaked, as she realized she was lying in a strange bed, in a strange room, with two strange people standing at the foot of the bed looking at her.

The two at the foot of the bed exchanged concerned looks with each other, and then turned back to look again at Vickie sitting up in the bed.

"I know you!" Vickie said as recognition dawned. "You've been in my dreams a lot lately. Well that explains this strange room. I must not be awake yet. I must still be dreaming."

"No, you are awake and not dreaming," the girl said with a gentle smile.

"I'm not dreaming?" Vickie questioned with a touch of panic in her voice.

"No, you dream not, though you are quite safe now," the older girl continued in a calming voice. "And by the word, I am so glad you are awake. You gave us a scare."

"A scare?" queried the still sleepy girl with a tinge of fear. "What kind of scare?"

The older girl glanced at the boy, and took a step forward. She leaned closer to the young girl and gently touched her foot. Somehow, the touch helped to calm Vickie's panic.

"Do you remember the house in the land of dreams?" asked the older girl. "And do you remember Micah coming to our rescue?"

Vickie glanced quickly from the girl to the boy, and then scrunched up her nose as she tried to recall her most recent memories. Suddenly, as if someone had been turning controls on a camera, the memories came into full focus.

Vickie gulped at the overwhelming flood and tried to sort out the details of her memories. "How much of what I remember was a dream, and how much was real?"

The boy stepped a little closer. "Shanti and I have had a similar experience as you, and we have been discussing that very question. We know we were in the land of dreams, so I do not think that much of what happened was real."

"Was any of it real?" questioned Vickie.

The older girl, Shanti, nodded her head. "We were trapped in the land of dreams, that did indeed happen."

"And we must tell you," continued Micah, "that after our escape from the land of dreams, you collapsed. You have slept for three full days."

"Well that would explain my achy muscles," Vickie said with a nod.

Then gathering her courage, Vickie asked the boy and girl standing before her, "So...exactly where am I?"

Micah smiled. "You are in a vacant dorm room at my school."

"In a dorm room," Vickie asked in confusion, "of your school?"

"Yes, my school, which is an all boys' school," Micah continued with a shy smile. "I was able to keep your presence a secret thus far, but we must get you back to your family before someone needs this room and you are discovered."

"Micah and I have talked much while you slept," Shanti said with a smile. "We have found that my village is not far from here, so I will be able to go home very easily."

"Much of what happened in the land of dreams is vague to me," continued Micah with a grimace, "so I cannot recall from what village you hail. I suspect that your home also cannot be far away. As soon as you tell us the name of your village, we can get you back to your people."

"You confuse me, with all this village stuff," groaned Vickie with a frown. "Nobody lives in villages, at least not in America. Everybody lives in towns, or cities, or the suburbs. Tell me the truth...have we left the United States? Are we out of the country?"

Her eyes finally acclimated to the bright light; Vickie opened them fully for the first time. As she turned her hazel eyes toward Micah, Vickie was surprised to see him suddenly turn pale and to hear his gasp of surprise.

"No," Micah whispered in shock, "it cannot be true."

Micah's mind had been in turmoil the last three days, with his emotional self arguing that the dreams were reality, while his logical self scoffed that they were pure imagination. His logical self had finally won the arguments, and Micah had accepted that all his recent adventures had merely been dreams.

There was no such thing as dream travel. And though he did believe he had been somehow trapped in the land of dreams along with these two girls, he really did not believe there was another world besides his own.

But all the arguments put forth by his logical self flew out the window with one look into Vickie's eyes.

Eyes like Vickie's could not happen in Micah's world. They were more than rare—they were absolutely impossible.

Except for rare instances where a blue eye and a brown eye married, blue eyes married blue eyes, brown eyes married brown eyes, green eyes married green eyes, and gray eyes married gray eyes. It had been that way for thousands of years.

It was custom, and it was law. Thus the purity of the birth gift was protected. And though there were the occasional oddities born with one brown eye and one blue eye like Shanti and Micah, there were never children born with eyes of mixed colors like Vickie's.

Micah felt the world tilt as he came to terms with the fact that logic was wrong, and it had not been simply a dream. He had traveled to another world, and this girl was from that world.

"By the word, we do have a problem," Micah said to Shanti after he sucked in a deep calming breath.

Shanti looked at him in surprise.

Micah sighed. "This girl is not a part of our world, look at her eyes!"

Shanti moved to the bedside and gently turned Vickie's face so she could get a better look at her eyes. Releasing Vickie's chin, she raised her own chin, closed her eyes, and took a slow deep breath, crinkling her forehead as if she were in great pain.

Shanti, like Micah, had convinced herself that she had just experienced a long strange dream. She had pushed the question of how she had come to be in a boys' dorm out of her consciousness. She had ignored the fact that she felt a friendship with two people she knew she had never met in her life. She did not want to find that her dream contained any truth.

It was not a question of logic versus emotion for Shanti. She had a much deeper reason to want what she remembered to simply be figments of her imagination.

For, if her memories were not simply harmless dreams where no guilt was ever attached to actions, she was guilty of causing real harm to this girl. She had helped Roland kidnap Vickie in the land of dreams. She had been a weak pawn in the hands of an evil man.

Vickie's eyes showed Shanti the truth. Because eyes of so many colors were impossible in Shanti's world, the dreams must not be imagination, but reality. Helping Roland, visiting the other world, being trapped in a room, going through the door to get home...they must all be true.

"You are right, she does not belong in our world," Shanti agreed with a sigh.

Micah threw his shoulders back, and remembered that by the Rite of Passage, he was now a man. He must act in a manly fashion.

"I am responsible for bringing her to this world, and I pledge to return her to her own." Micah vowed to Shanti.

"I also share in that responsibility, probably more so than you," Shanti responded, pinning Micah with a glare. "I do not shirk my duties, so I will undertake to get this girl home."

"This is a job for a man. I—" began Micah.

"I take this girl as my little sister," interrupted Shanti. "Therefore I am responsible—"

"No, you cannot! As a man I must protect this girl and—"

"As her sister I am entitled to help this girl—"

"Why thanks guys, I am glad you both care. But 'this girl' isn't some toy that needs to be returned to its owner," Vickie said firmly, interrupting the full-scale battle that was about to ensue. "What exactly do you mean by 'this world'? Am I in another country? Is that what you mean by 'this world'?"

"You are in a land called Braumaru, the Land of the Four Sisters," Micah said with a tentative smile. He was a little ashamed of himself for forgetting that 'this girl' could think and act for herself.

Shanti continued the explanation, "We are not sure exactly what has happened. I do know that I went to sleep one night, and I seemed to keep dreaming for a very long time. I met a man named Roland, he took me to see you, I met Micah, I traveled all over a strange world, I was trapped with you in a house, Micah came...and the next thing I knew, I was here."

Micah jumped in with what he felt was the most important point, "We believe that we have been traveling in our dreams, and that it is through dream travel that you have been brought here from your world."

Vickie still looked confused. "So there is that word again 'world'. What do you mean 'your world'?"

"By the word," began Micah with frustration, "I do not know how to explain!"

Shanti gently placed her hand on Micah's shoulder and faced Vickie. "We appear to come from different earths, or maybe different times. We seem to have found a way to pass from one earth to another, using our dreams."

"Wow," exclaimed Vickie in excitement. "You mean we have been time-traveling?"

"We do not know for sure if there is a difference in time," Shanti gently explained. "We just know there is little similar between your world and ours."

"This will be great for my book! I can just imagine how exciting the story will be—"

"Vickie, you must take this seriously," Micah interrupted. "You are in a world that is not your own. Your people do not know what has happened to you. You could be discovered in our world at any time, and I do not know how to explain your presence."

"Micah is right," Shanti agreed. "We must get you back to your world as soon as we can."

"Well no problem," said Vickie. "I'll just go back to sleep and travel back home the same way I got here."

Shanti rolled her eyes. "You think it will be as easy as that? You will just go to sleep and all will be well?"

"Why not?" shrugged Vickie. "If I got here in a dream, I should be able to go home in a dream. So good night, it was nice meeting you, and I'm ready to wake up in my own bed now."

"I do not think it will be that easy to get you home," said Micah shaking his head.

"Why not," asked Vickie with a frown as she sat back up in the bed.

"Vickie," explained Shanti, "we were trapped for days in that house. If Micah had not found us, I think we would have died."

"It wouldn't really matter if we died in the dream!" laughed Vickie. "If you die in a dream, you don't really die. That is just an old wives' tale. My mama said so."

"You do not understand. Are you asleep now?" Micah asked gravely.

"No, of course not," responded Vickie with a smile.

"How know you for certain?" queried Shanti.

"I know when I am really asleep, and really awake. See," she said as she pinched her arm as hard as she could, "ouch, that hurts! I am most definitely awake."

"So how did you get here?" Shanti asked gently.

"Well you said I got here through a dream."

"Yes," Shanti continued calmly, "and dreams are ever hard to control. I must stress, we do not know exactly how we got you here!"

"But if I go back to sleep and dream of home—"

"It must take more than just dreaming of a place," interrupted Micah, "otherwise Shanti would not have been trapped with Roland. She could have gotten back home by herself."

"Shanti was trapped? Where?"

"I was trapped in your world," Shanti explained. "I found I needed to trust a man my instinct told me not to trust, because I was unable to dream myself back home."

"You tried, more than once?"

"Many times," Shanti answered sadly.

"It took the three of us together to get back to our world," Micah explained. "And you were very sick by the time we got you here."

"If you had stayed much longer in the land of dreams," Shanti said with a shiver, "you would not have survived."

Micah nodded his head. "We cannot take the chance that any of us will become trapped again. We must find more knowledge about dream travel."

"And," Shanti added firmly as she looked at the dark circles under Vickie's eyes, "we must give you time to get strong again before you attempt the journey."

"But I can't stay in a boy's dorm," Vickie cried out in horror. "Isn't there somewhere else we can go while I recuperate?"

A grin spread across Micah's face as the answer to their most immediate problem popped into his head. "Cerulea," he said happily.

"Cerulea" questioned Shanti, "the Land of the Eyes of Blue?"

"Yes," replied Micah. "My family has rooms there where we might stay. My father will approve of the journey, for he is always suggesting that I go to visit."

"Yes," reluctantly agreed Shanti, "it would be a very good place for Vickie to get well again. But a journey, in her weakened condition—"

Micah's grin widened as he waited for Shanti to realize the brilliance of his plan. "Yes, a journey to Cerulea will be perfect. It is not only called the Land of the Eyes of Blue, you know."

Vickie confusedly looked first at Shanti, then to Micah, and back again to Shanti, trying to figure out the strange undercurrents swirling between those two. She had just shifted her gaze again to Shanti when she saw enlightenment dawn on her face.

"Perfect indeed," agreed Shanti with a smile. "A trip to the City of Knowledge will indeed be just what we need."

And so the adventure begins.

Made in the USA
Lexington, KY
20 December 2011